5/10

THE INVISIBLE MAN

Adapted by
Joeming Dunn

Illustrated by
Ben Dunn

Based upon the works of
H.G. Wells

magic
Wagon

visit us at
www.abdopublishing.com

Published by Magic Wagon, a division of the ABDO Group, 8000 West 78th Street, Edina, Minnesota 55439. Copyright © 2010 by Abdo Consulting Group, Inc. International copyrights reserved in all countries. All rights reserved. No part of this book may be reproduced in any form without written permission from the publisher.

Graphic Planet™ is a trademark and logo of Magic Wagon.

Printed in the United States.

 Manufactured with paper containing at least 10% post-consumer waste

Original novel by H.G. Wells
Adapted and lettered by Joeming Dunn
Illustrated by Ben Dunn
Colored by Robby Bevard and Lee Duhig
Edited by Stephanie Hedlund and Rochelle Baltzer
Interior layout and design by Antarctic Press
Cover art by Ben Dunn
Cover design by Neil Klinepier

Library of Congress Cataloging-in-Publication Data

Dunn, Joeming.
    The Invisible Man / H.G. Wells; adapted by Joeming Dunn and illustrated by Ben Dunn ; based upon the works of H.G. Wells.
    p. cm. -- (Graphic planet. Graphic horror)
    Summary: A graphic novel based on the H.G. Wells classic, in which a quiet English country village is disturbed by the arrival of a mysterious stranger who keeps his face hidden and his back to everyone.
    ISBN 978-1-60270-677-4 (alk. paper)
    1. Graphic novels. [1. Graphic novels. 2. Wells, H. G. (Herbert George), 1866-1946. Invisible man--Adaptations. 3. Science fiction.] I. Dunn, Ben, ill. II. Wells, H. G. (Herbert George), 1866-1946. Invisible man. III. Title.

PZ7.7.D86Inv 2010
741.5'973--dc22

        2009008587

TABLE OF CONTENTS

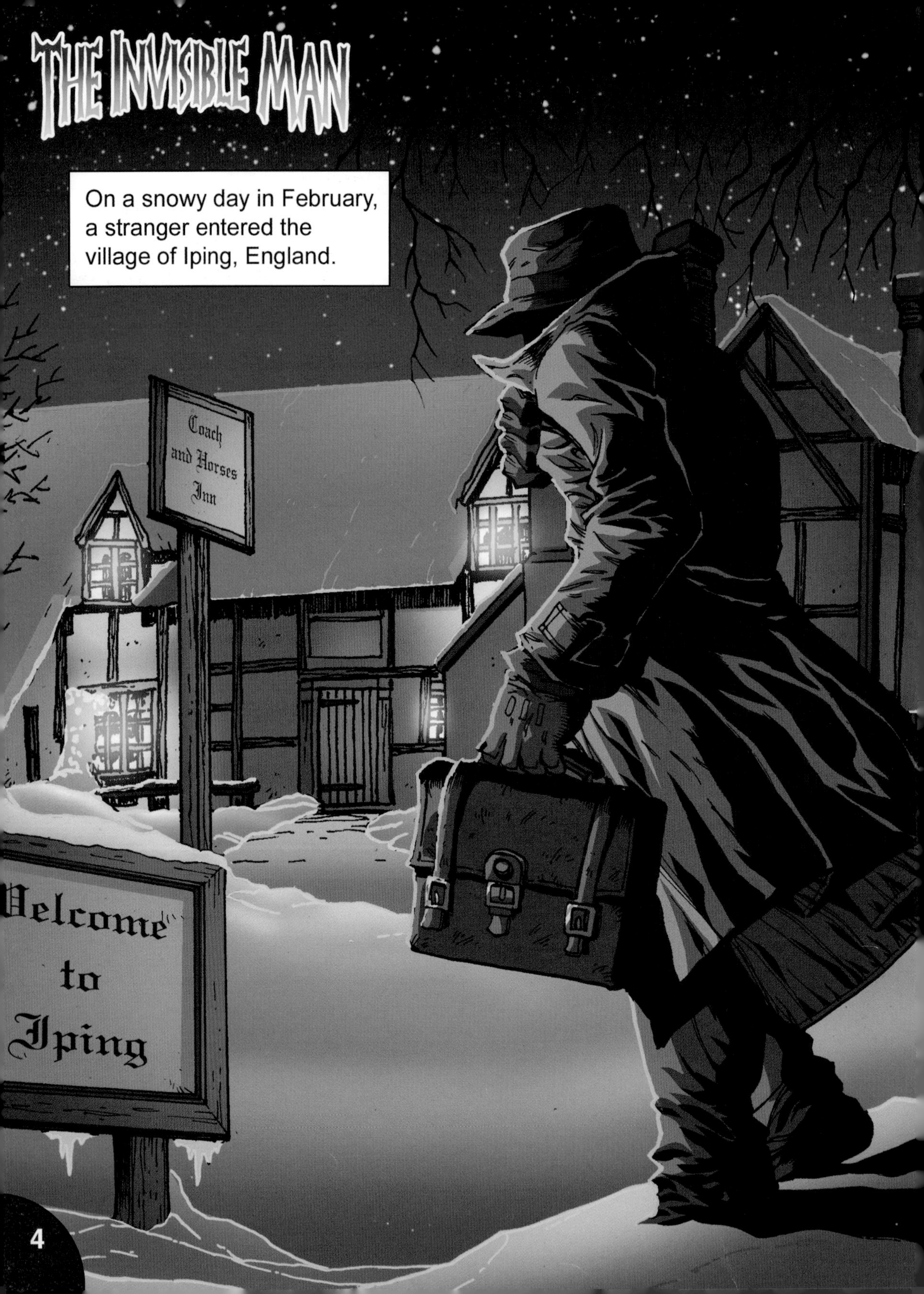
THE INVISIBLE MAN
On a snowy day in February, a stranger entered the village of Iping, England.
Coach and Horses Inn
Welcome to Iping

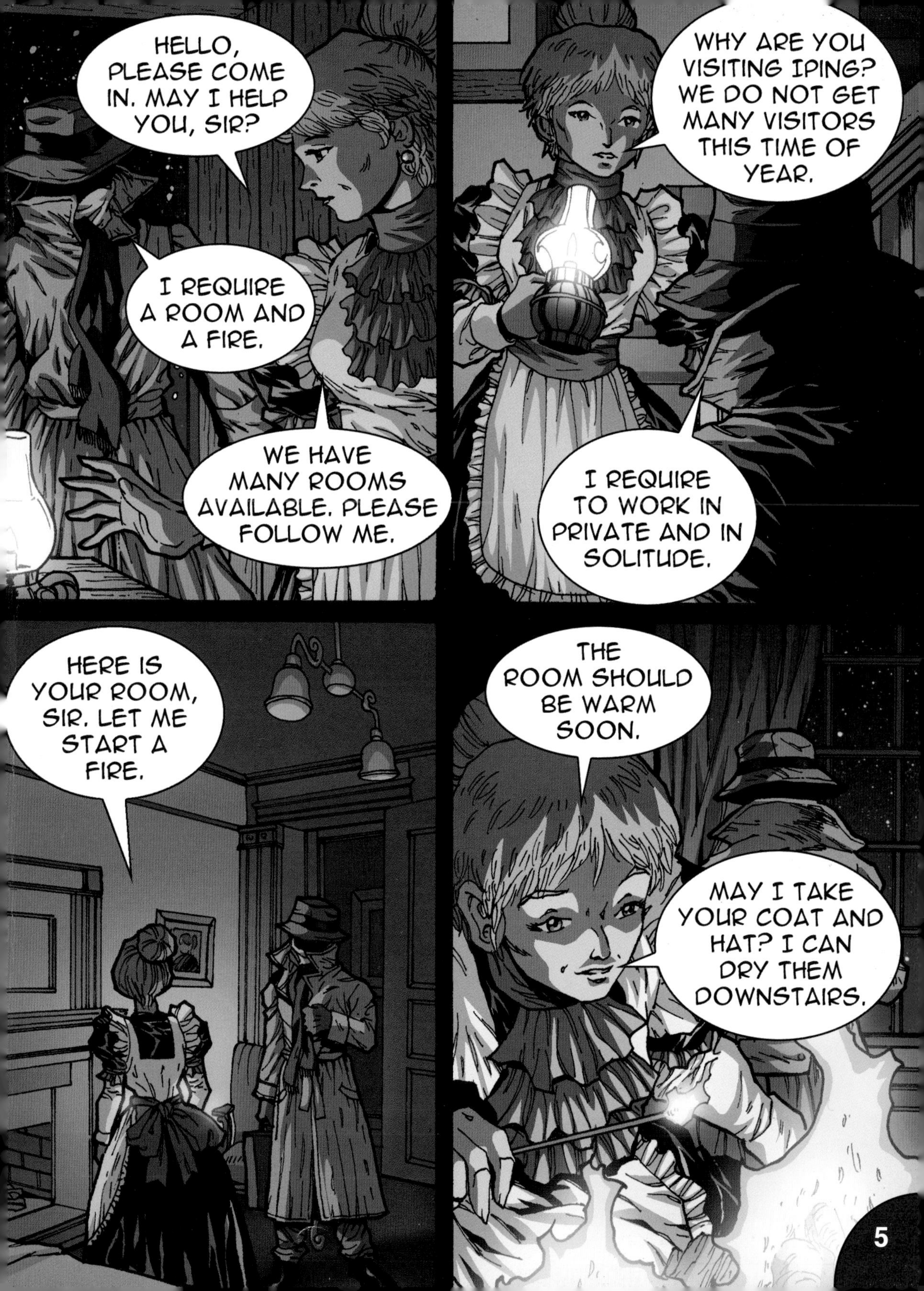
HELLO, PLEASE COME IN. MAY I HELP YOU, SIR?
I REQUIRE A ROOM AND A FIRE.
WE HAVE MANY ROOMS AVAILABLE. PLEASE FOLLOW ME.
WHY ARE YOU VISITING IPING? WE DO NOT GET MANY VISITORS THIS TIME OF YEAR.
I REQUIRE TO WORK IN PRIVATE AND IN SOLITUDE.
HERE IS YOUR ROOM, SIR. LET ME START A FIRE.
THE ROOM SHOULD BE WARM SOON.
MAY I TAKE YOUR COAT AND HAT? I CAN DRY THEM DOWNSTAIRS.

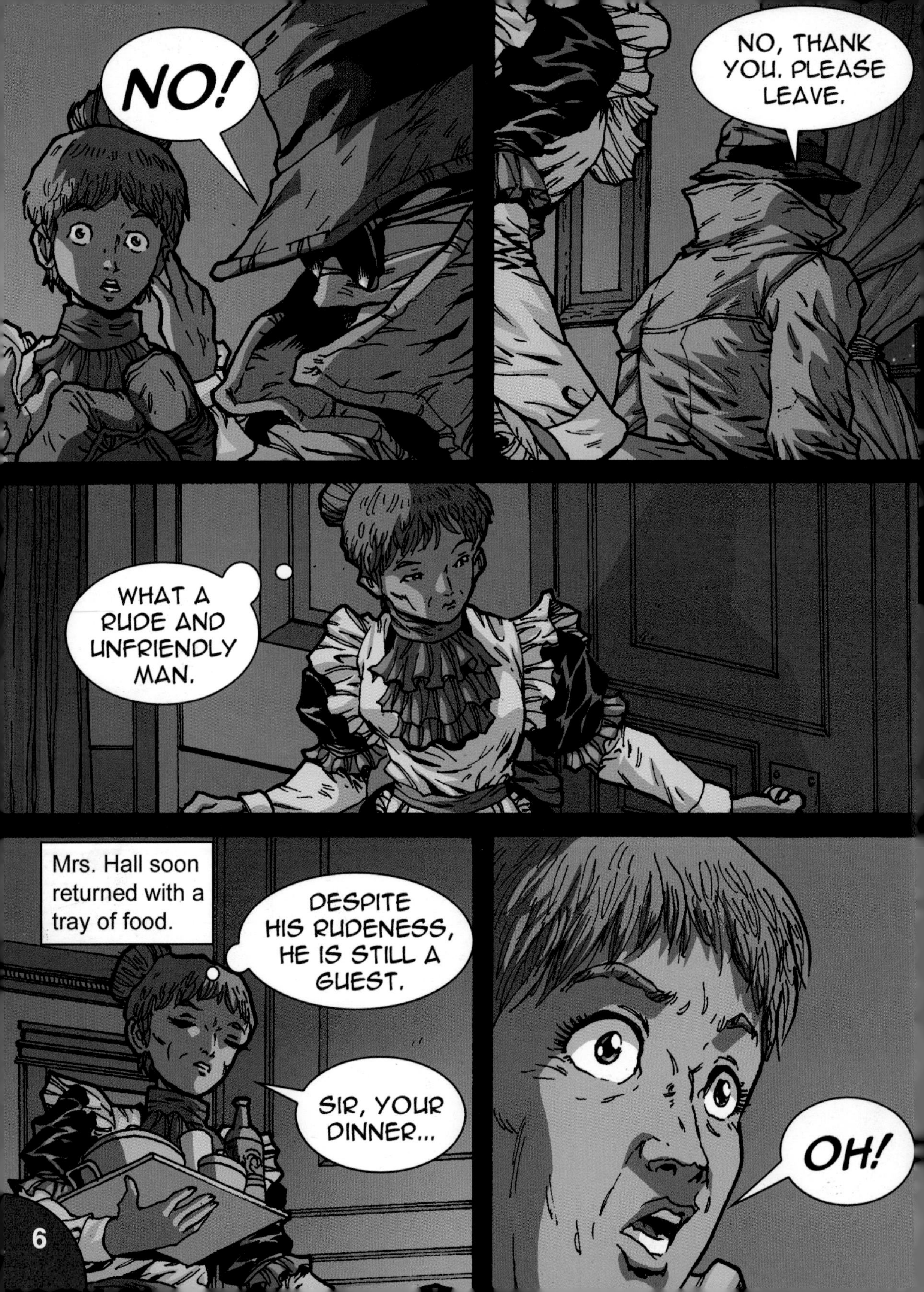
NO!
NO, THANK YOU. PLEASE LEAVE.
WHAT A RUDE AND UNFRIENDLY MAN.
Mrs. Hall soon returned with a tray of food.
DESPITE HIS RUDENESS, HE IS STILL A GUEST.
SIR, YOUR DINNER...
OH!

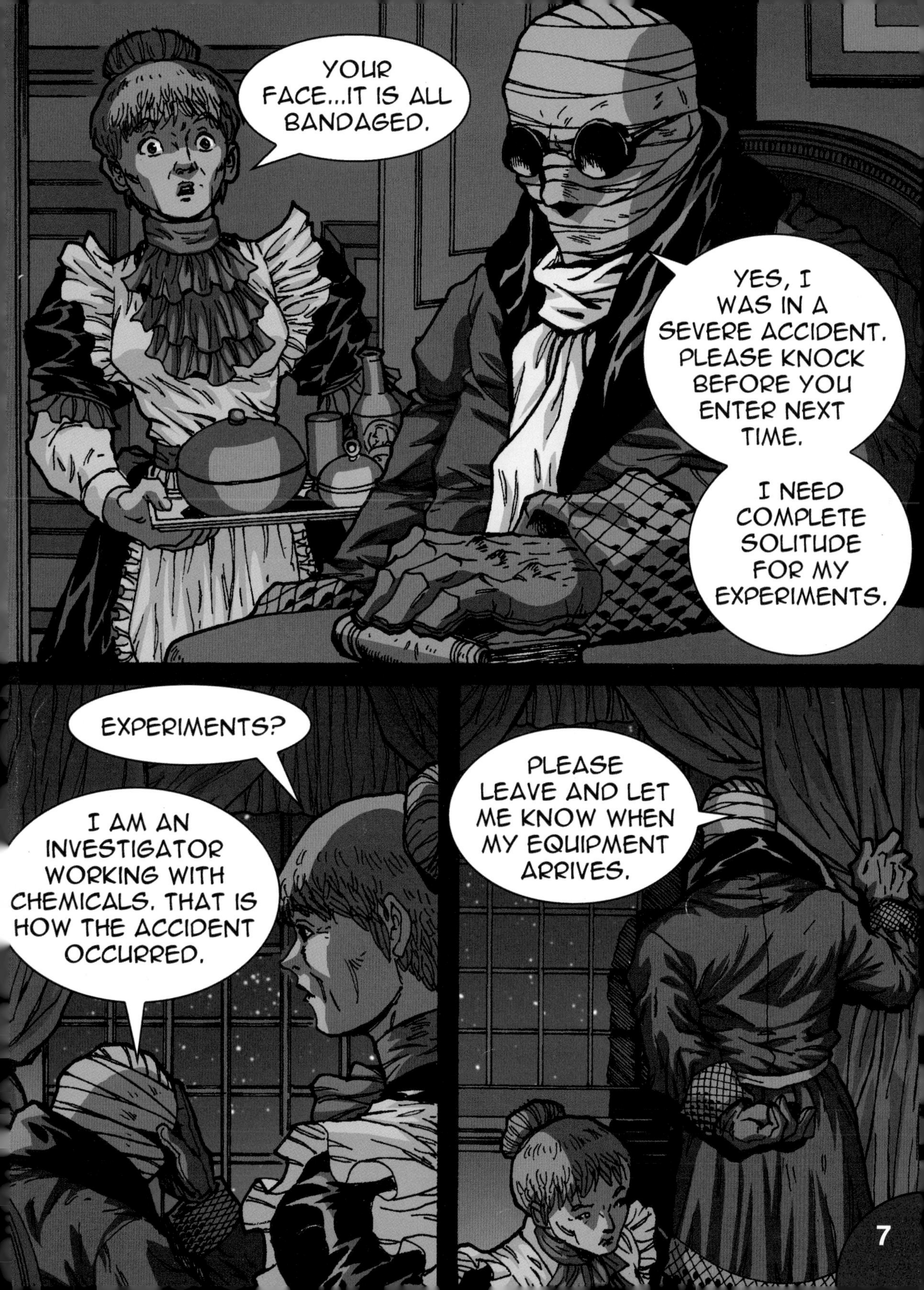
YOUR FACE...IT IS ALL BANDAGED.
YES, I WAS IN A SEVERE ACCIDENT. PLEASE KNOCK BEFORE YOU ENTER NEXT TIME.
I NEED COMPLETE SOLITUDE FOR MY EXPERIMENTS.
EXPERIMENTS?
I AM AN INVESTIGATOR WORKING WITH CHEMICALS. THAT IS HOW THE ACCIDENT OCCURRED.
PLEASE LEAVE AND LET ME KNOW WHEN MY EQUIPMENT ARRIVES.

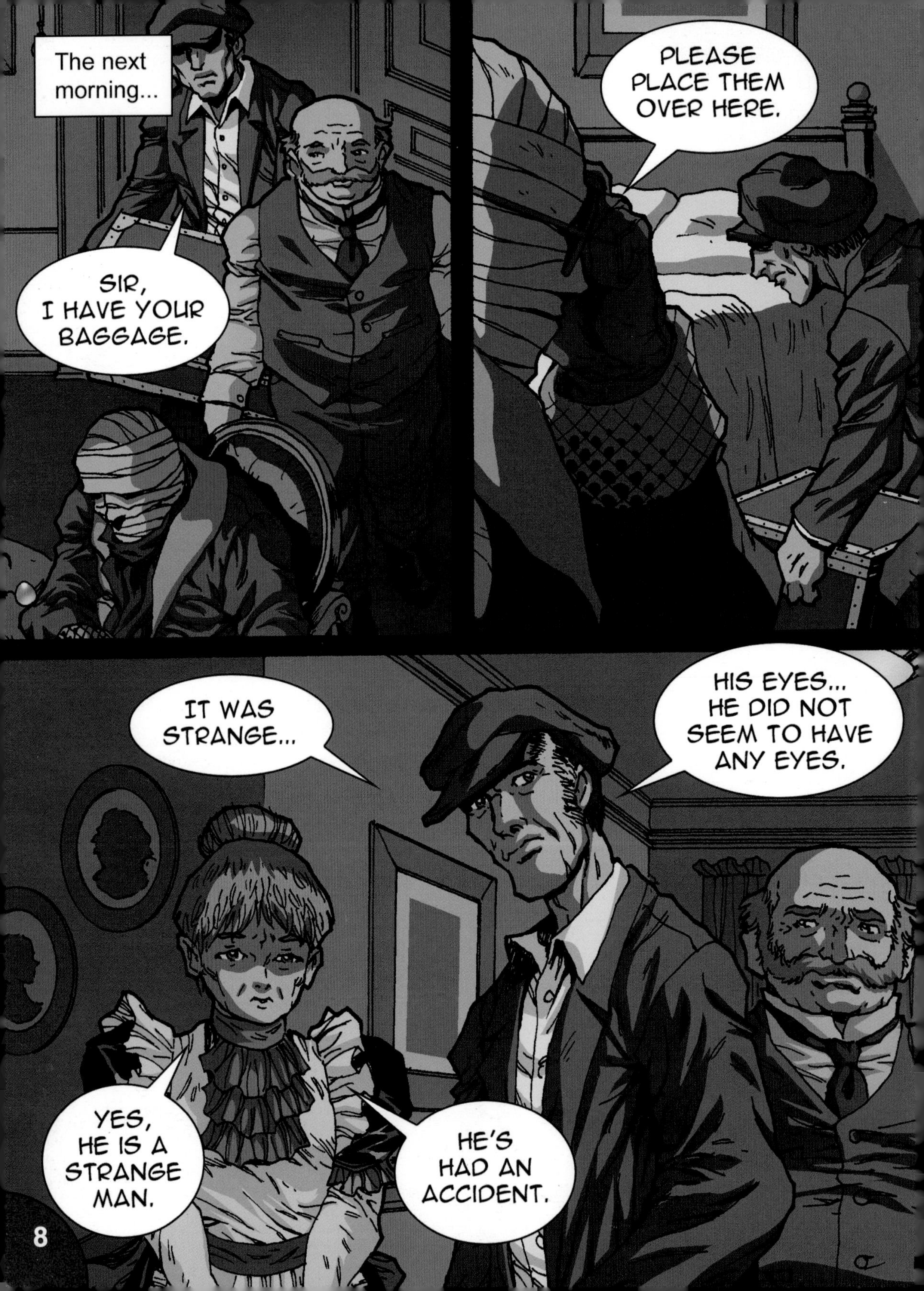
The next morning...
SIR, I HAVE YOUR BAGGAGE.
PLEASE PLACE THEM OVER HERE.
IT WAS STRANGE...
HIS EYES... HE DID NOT SEEM TO HAVE ANY EYES.
YES, HE IS A STRANGE MAN.
HE'S HAD AN ACCIDENT.

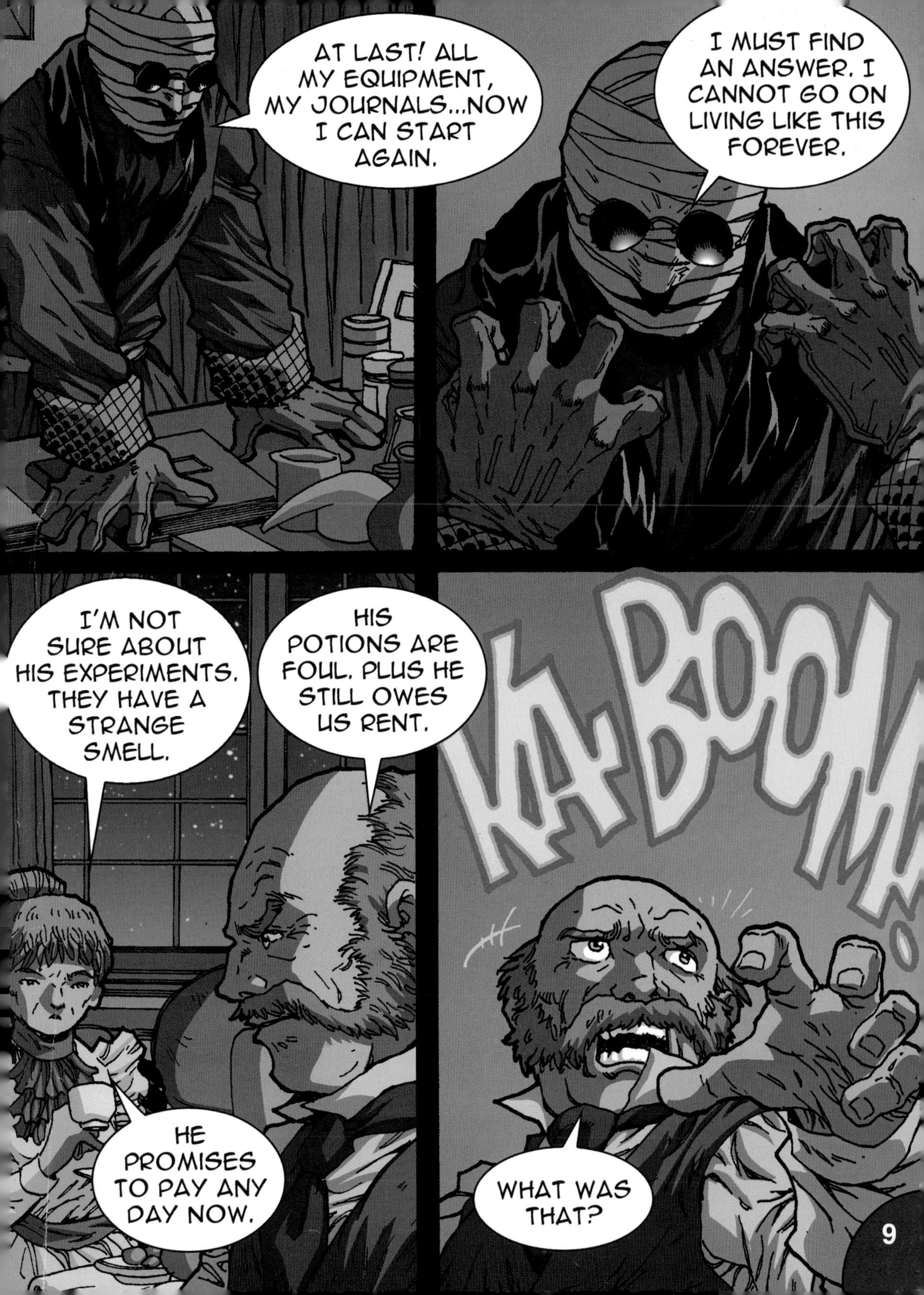
AT LAST! ALL MY EQUIPMENT, MY JOURNALS...NOW I CAN START AGAIN.
I MUST FIND AN ANSWER. I CANNOT GO ON LIVING LIKE THIS FOREVER.
I'M NOT SURE ABOUT HIS EXPERIMENTS. THEY HAVE A STRANGE SMELL.
HIS POTIONS ARE FOUL. PLUS HE STILL OWES US RENT.
HE PROMISES TO PAY ANY DAY NOW.
KA-BOOM!!
WHAT WAS THAT?

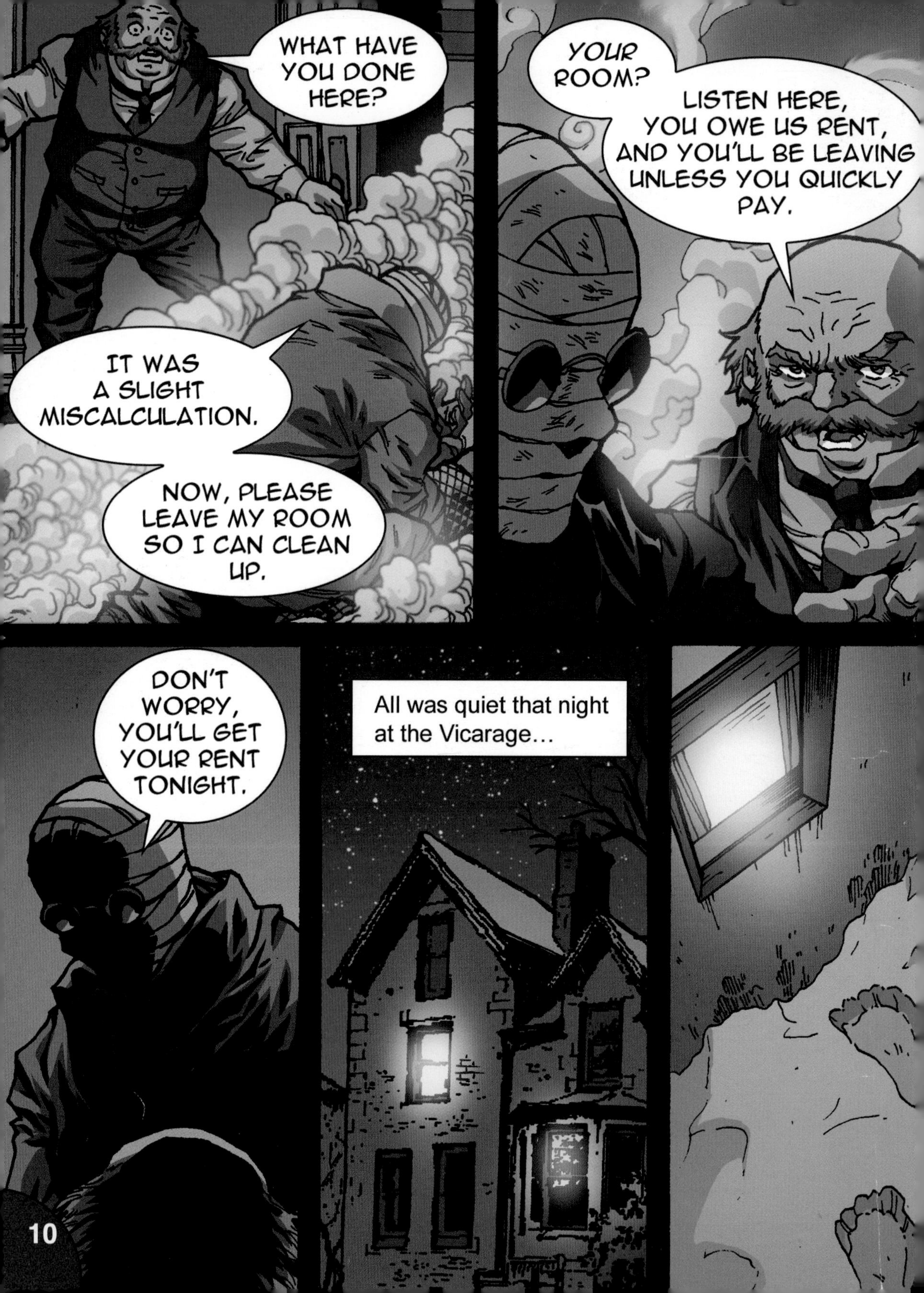
WHAT HAVE YOU DONE HERE?
IT WAS A SLIGHT MISCALCULATION.
NOW, PLEASE LEAVE MY ROOM SO I CAN CLEAN UP.
YOUR ROOM?
LISTEN HERE, YOU OWE US RENT, AND YOU'LL BE LEAVING UNLESS YOU QUICKLY PAY.
DON'T WORRY, YOU'LL GET YOUR RENT TONIGHT.
All was quiet that night at the Vicarage…

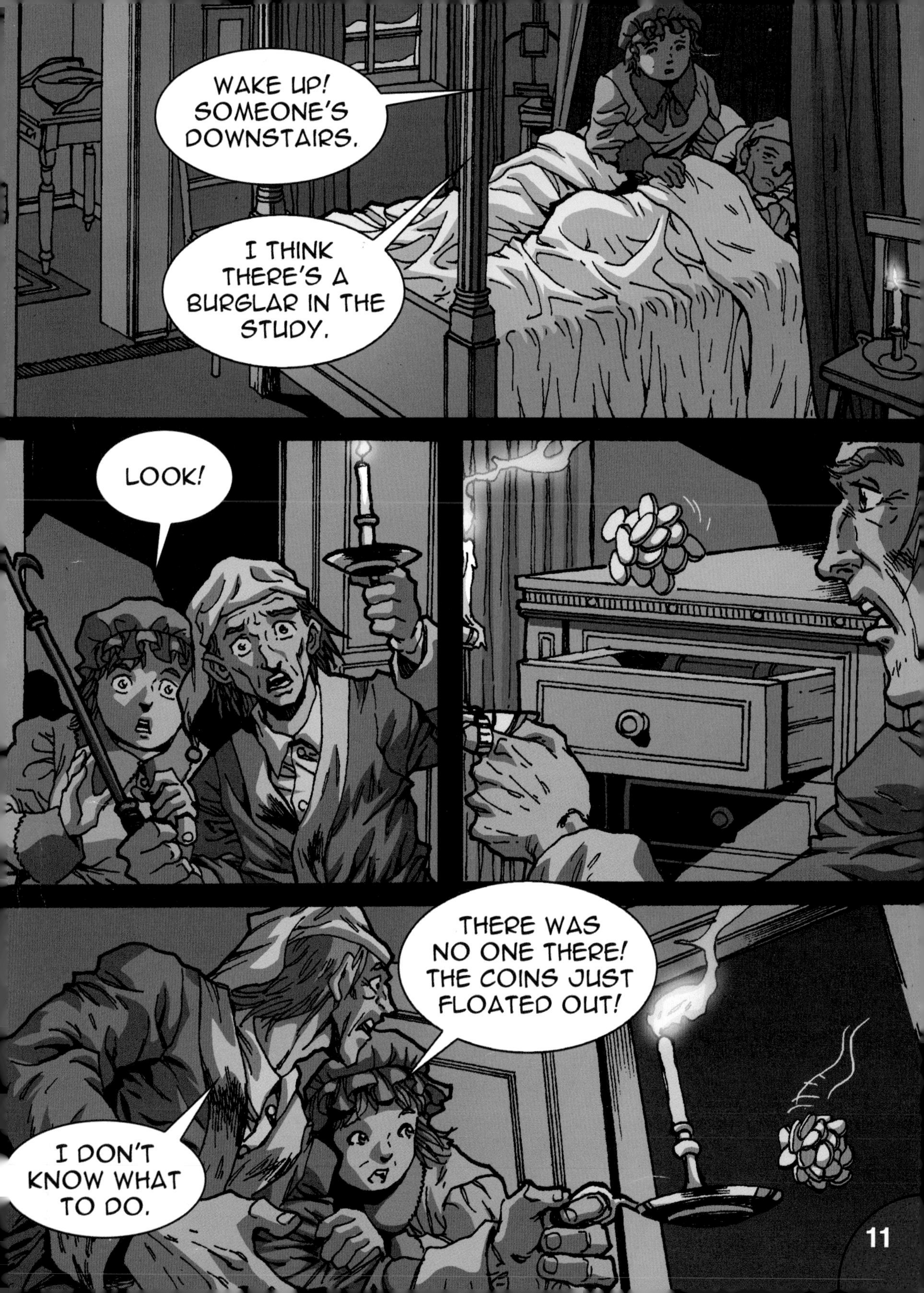
WAKE UP! SOMEONE'S DOWNSTAIRS.
I THINK THERE'S A BURGLAR IN THE STUDY.
LOOK!
THERE WAS NO ONE THERE! THE COINS JUST FLOATED OUT!
I DON'T KNOW WHAT TO DO.

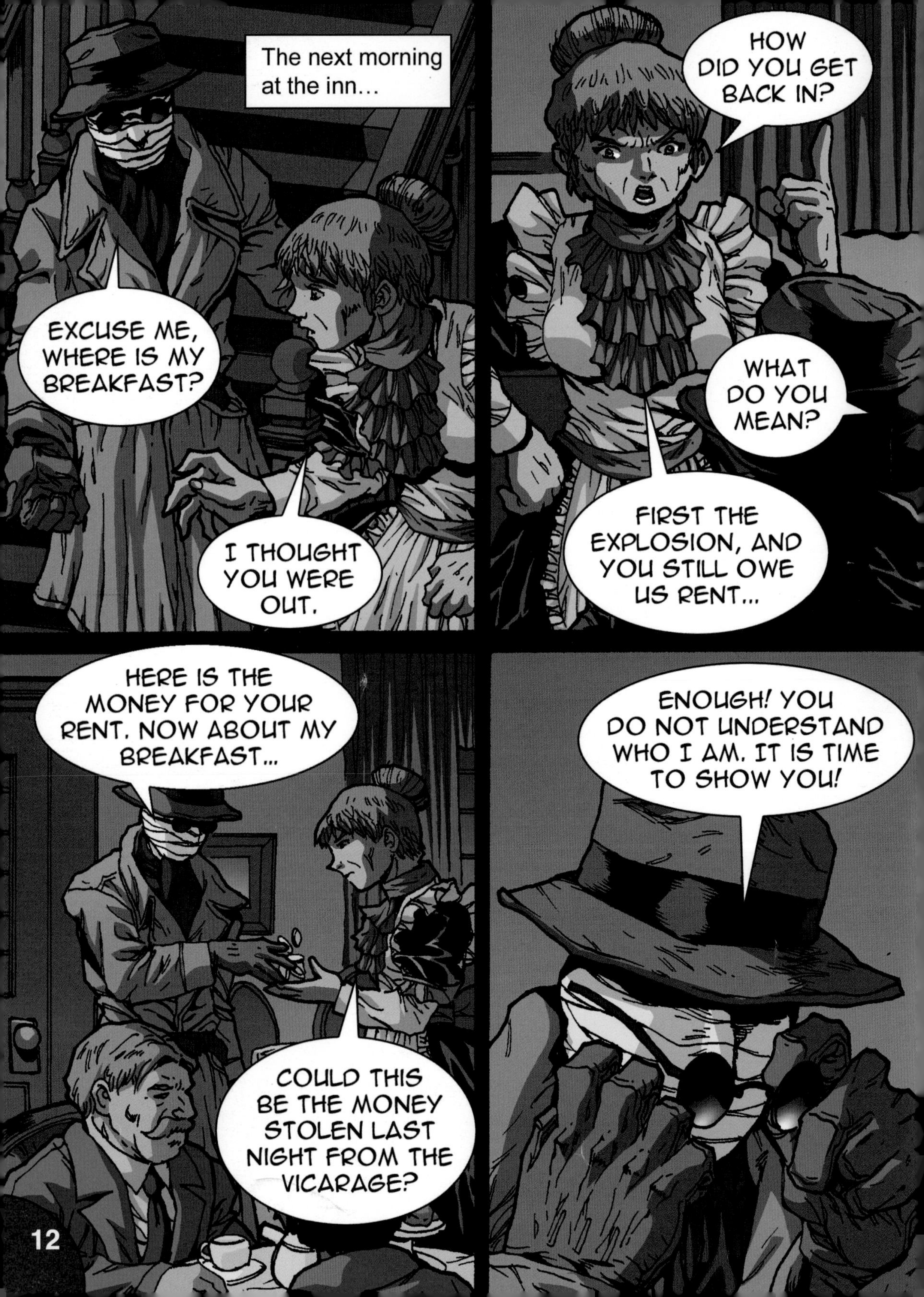

The next morning at the inn…
EXCUSE ME, WHERE IS MY BREAKFAST?
I THOUGHT YOU WERE OUT.
HOW DID YOU GET BACK IN?
WHAT DO YOU MEAN?
FIRST THE EXPLOSION, AND YOU STILL OWE US RENT...
HERE IS THE MONEY FOR YOUR RENT. NOW ABOUT MY BREAKFAST...
COULD THIS BE THE MONEY STOLEN LAST NIGHT FROM THE VICARAGE?
ENOUGH! YOU DO NOT UNDERSTAND WHO I AM. IT IS TIME TO SHOW YOU!

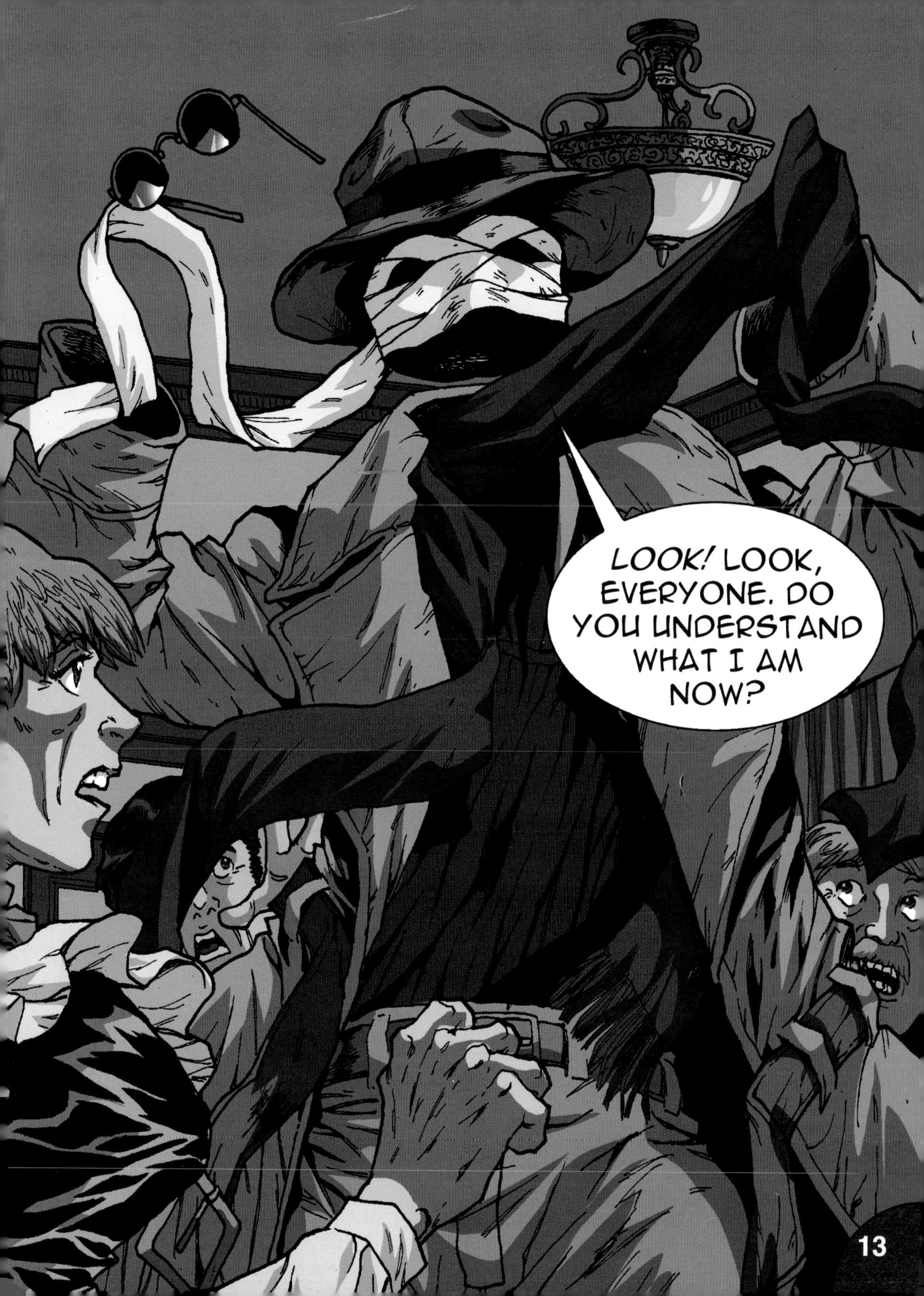
LOOK! LOOK, EVERYONE. DO YOU UNDERSTAND WHAT I AM NOW?

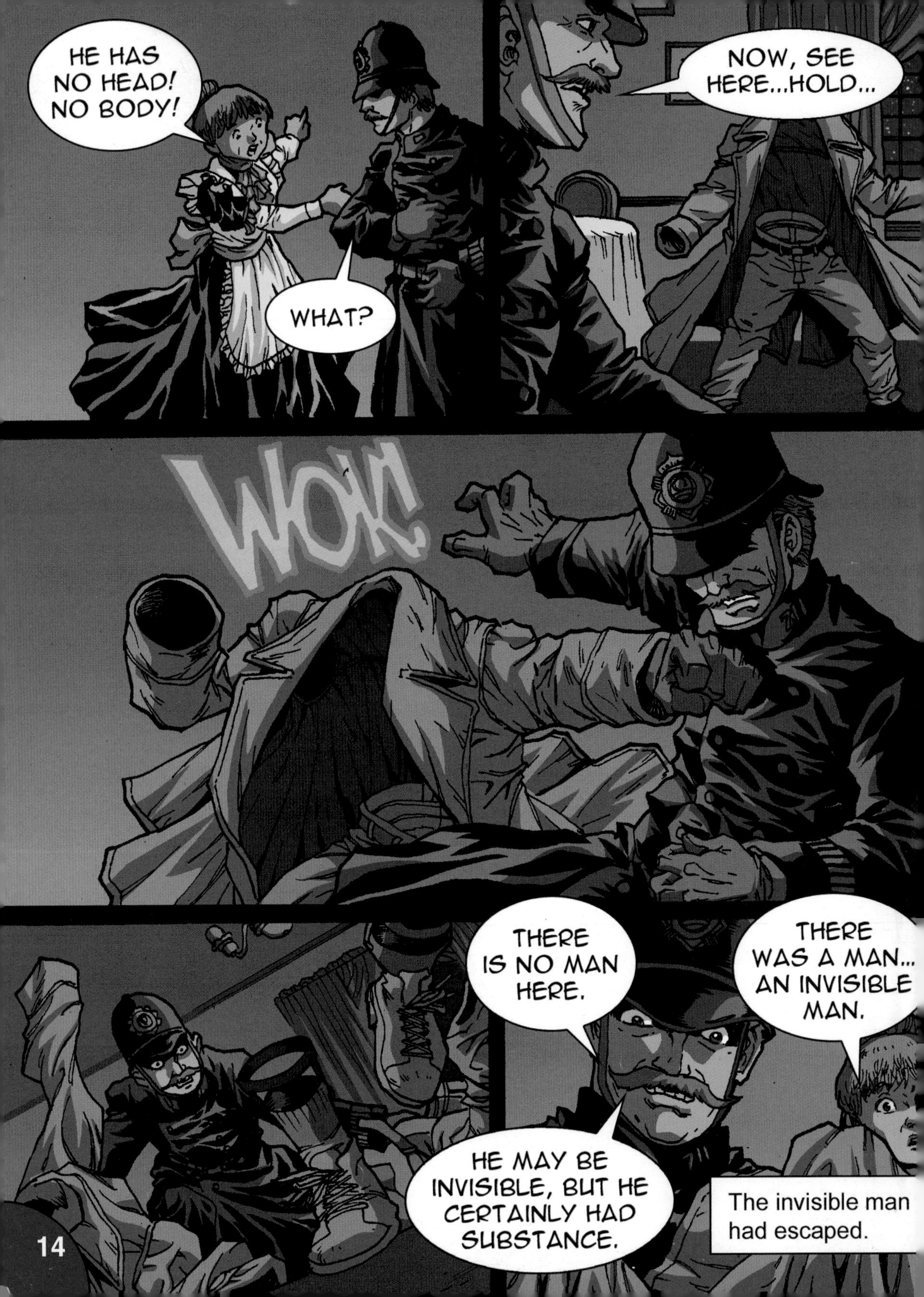
HE HAS NO HEAD! NO BODY!
WHAT?
NOW, SEE HERE...HOLD...
WOK!
THERE IS NO MAN HERE.
THERE WAS A MAN... AN INVISIBLE MAN.
HE MAY BE INVISIBLE, BUT HE CERTAINLY HAD SUBSTANCE.
The invisible man had escaped.

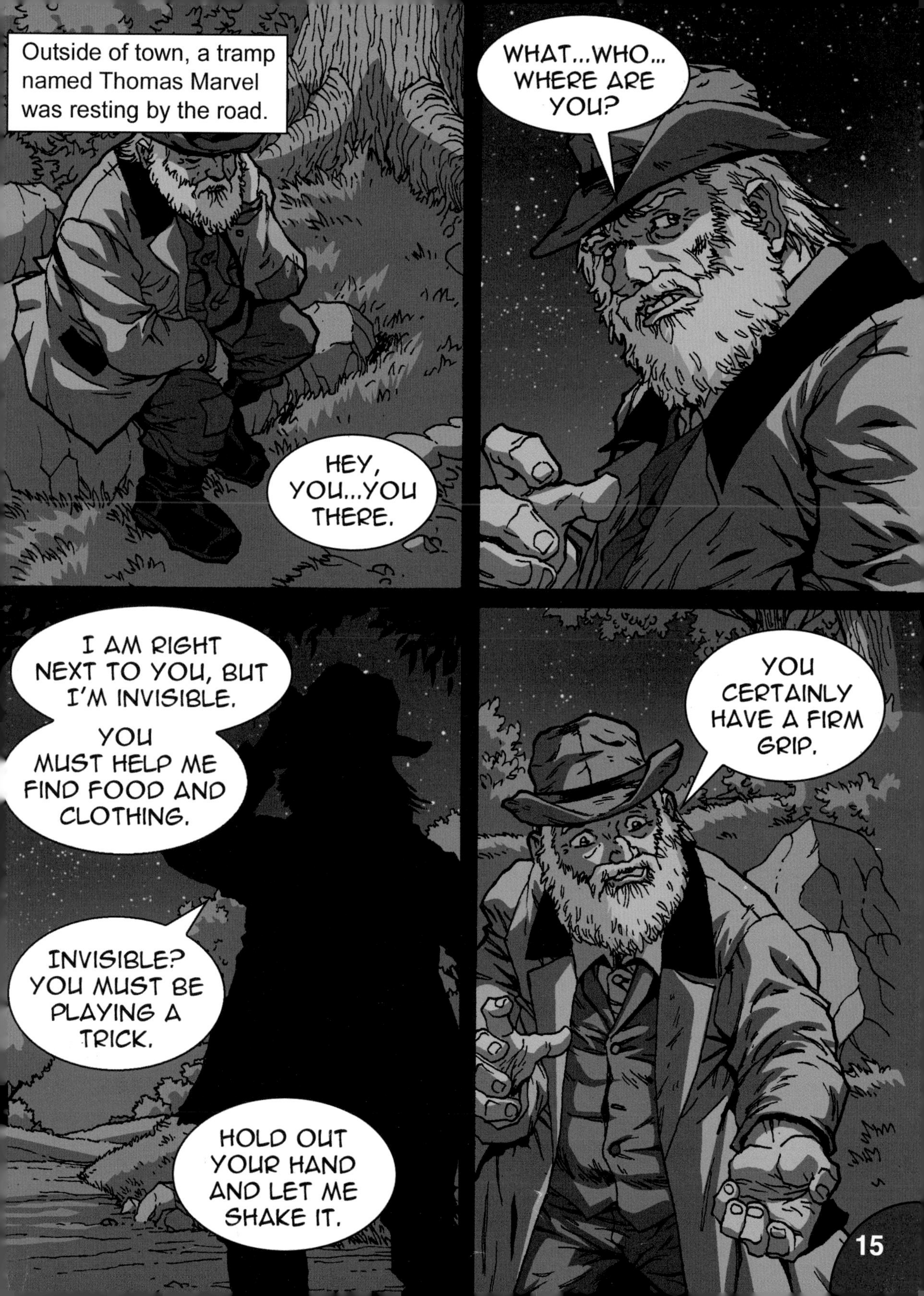
Outside of town, a tramp named Thomas Marvel was resting by the road.
HEY, YOU...YOU THERE.
WHAT...WHO... WHERE ARE YOU?
I AM RIGHT NEXT TO YOU, BUT I'M INVISIBLE.
YOU MUST HELP ME FIND FOOD AND CLOTHING.
INVISIBLE? YOU MUST BE PLAYING A TRICK.
HOLD OUT YOUR HAND AND LET ME SHAKE IT.
YOU CERTAINLY HAVE A FIRM GRIP.

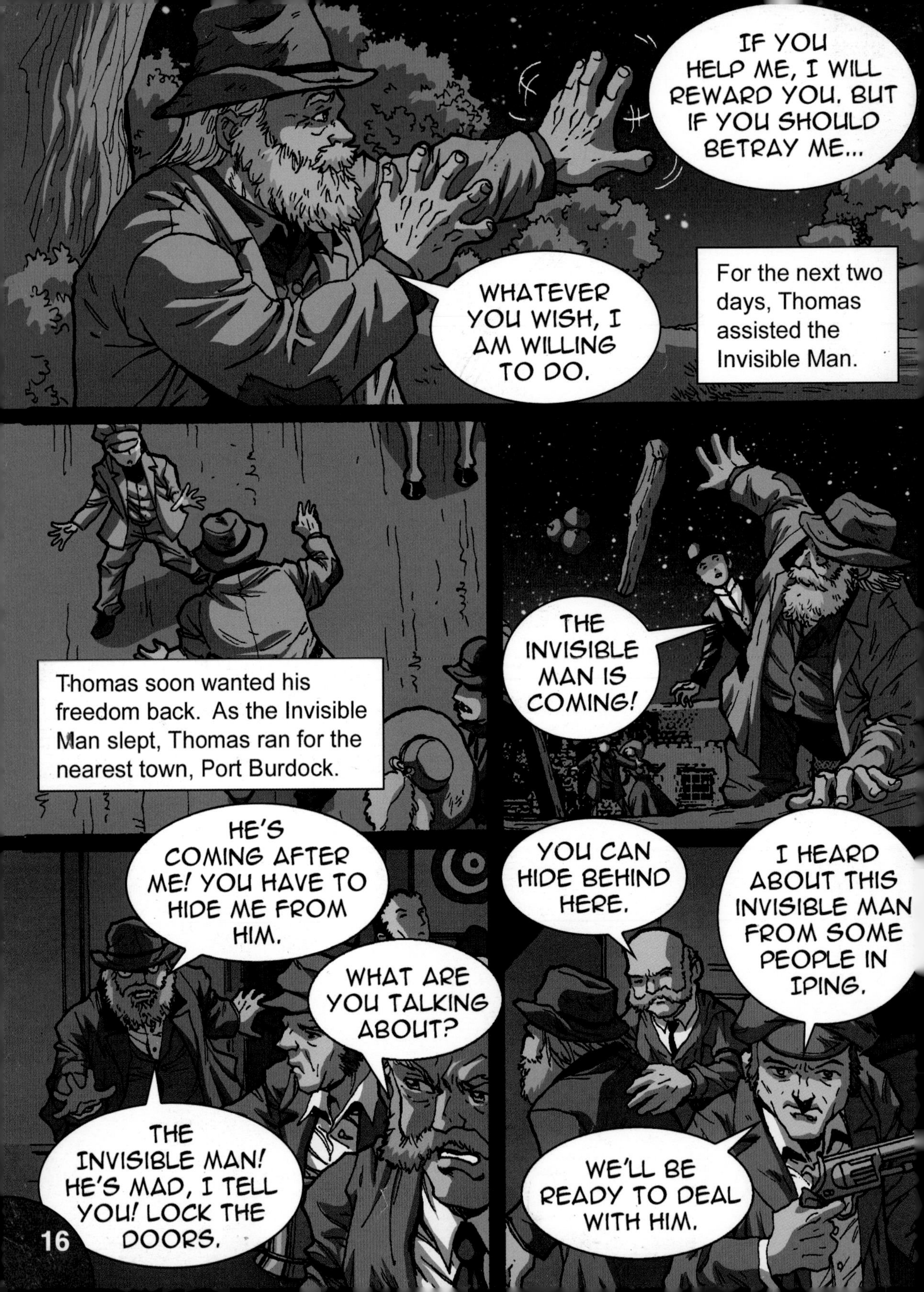
IF YOU HELP ME, I WILL REWARD YOU. BUT IF YOU SHOULD BETRAY ME...
WHATEVER YOU WISH, I AM WILLING TO DO.
For the next two days, Thomas assisted the Invisible Man.
Thomas soon wanted his freedom back. As the Invisible Man slept, Thomas ran for the nearest town, Port Burdock.
THE INVISIBLE MAN IS COMING!
HE'S COMING AFTER ME! YOU HAVE TO HIDE ME FROM HIM.
WHAT ARE YOU TALKING ABOUT?
THE INVISIBLE MAN! HE'S MAD, I TELL YOU! LOCK THE DOORS.
YOU CAN HIDE BEHIND HERE.
I HEARD ABOUT THIS INVISIBLE MAN FROM SOME PEOPLE IN IPING.
WE'LL BE READY TO DEAL WITH HIM.

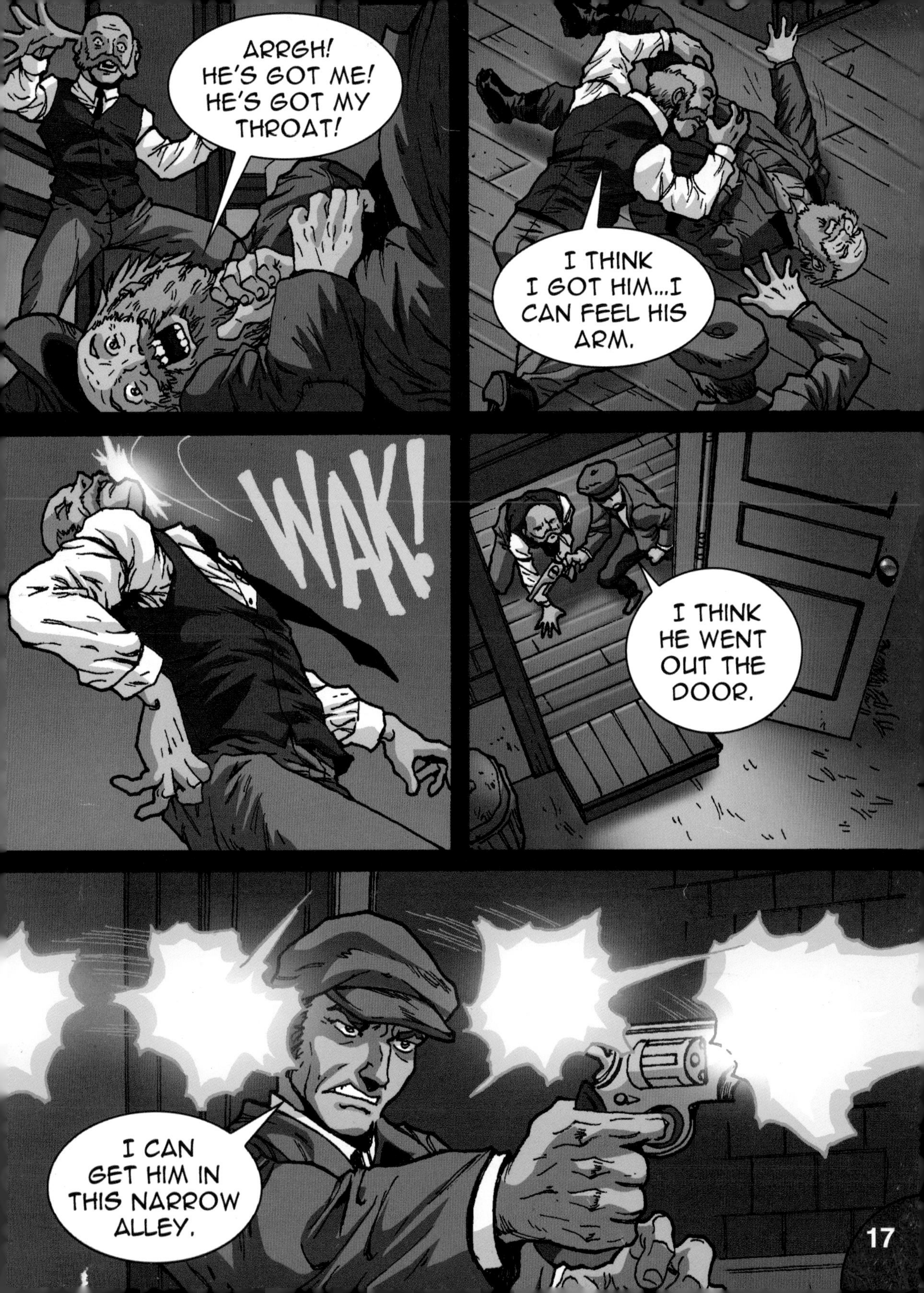
ARRGH! HE'S GOT ME! HE'S GOT MY THROAT!
I THINK I GOT HIM...I CAN FEEL HIS ARM.
WAK!
I THINK HE WENT OUT THE DOOR.
I CAN GET HIM IN THIS NARROW ALLEY.

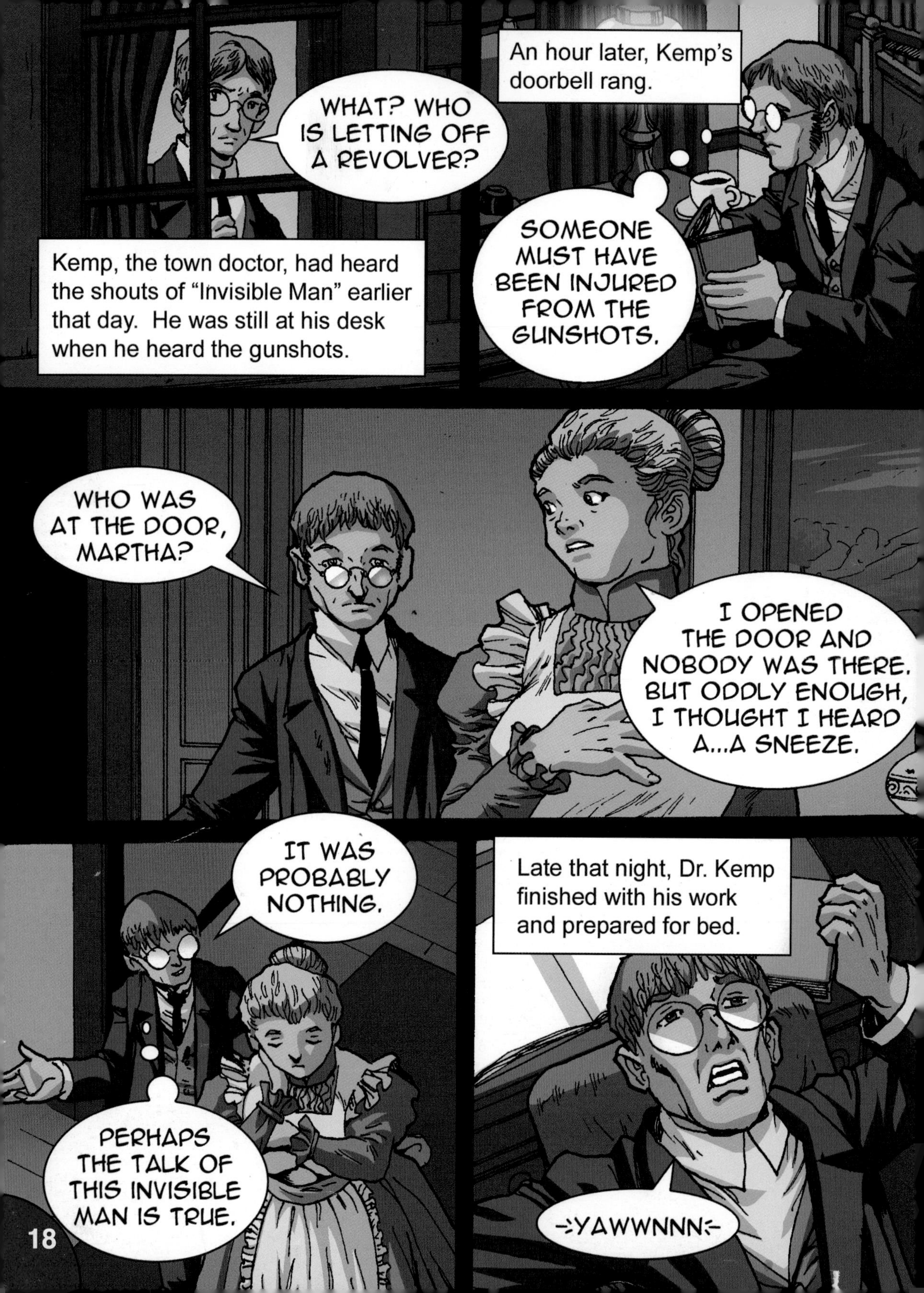

WHAT? WHO IS LETTING OFF A REVOLVER?
Kemp, the town doctor, had heard the shouts of "Invisible Man" earlier that day. He was still at his desk when he heard the gunshots.
An hour later, Kemp's doorbell rang.
SOMEONE MUST HAVE BEEN INJURED FROM THE GUNSHOTS.
WHO WAS AT THE DOOR, MARTHA?
I OPENED THE DOOR AND NOBODY WAS THERE. BUT ODDLY ENOUGH, I THOUGHT I HEARD A...A SNEEZE.
IT WAS PROBABLY NOTHING.
PERHAPS THE TALK OF THIS INVISIBLE MAN IS TRUE.
Late that night, Dr. Kemp finished with his work and prepared for bed.
-YAWWNNN-

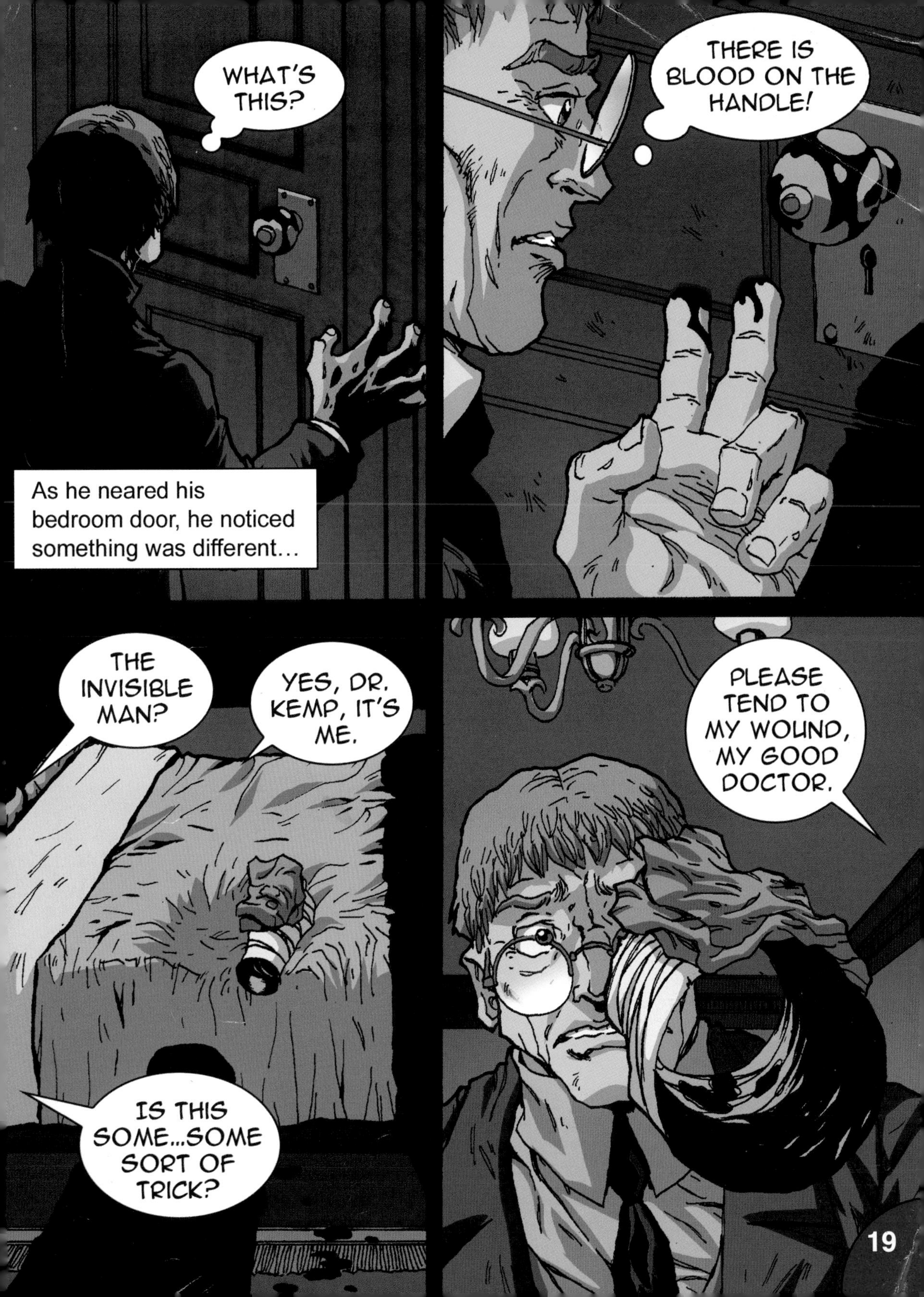
WHAT'S THIS?
As he neared his bedroom door, he noticed something was different…
THERE IS BLOOD ON THE HANDLE!
THE INVISIBLE MAN?
YES, DR. KEMP, IT'S ME.
IS THIS SOME...SOME SORT OF TRICK?
PLEASE TEND TO MY WOUND, MY GOOD DOCTOR.

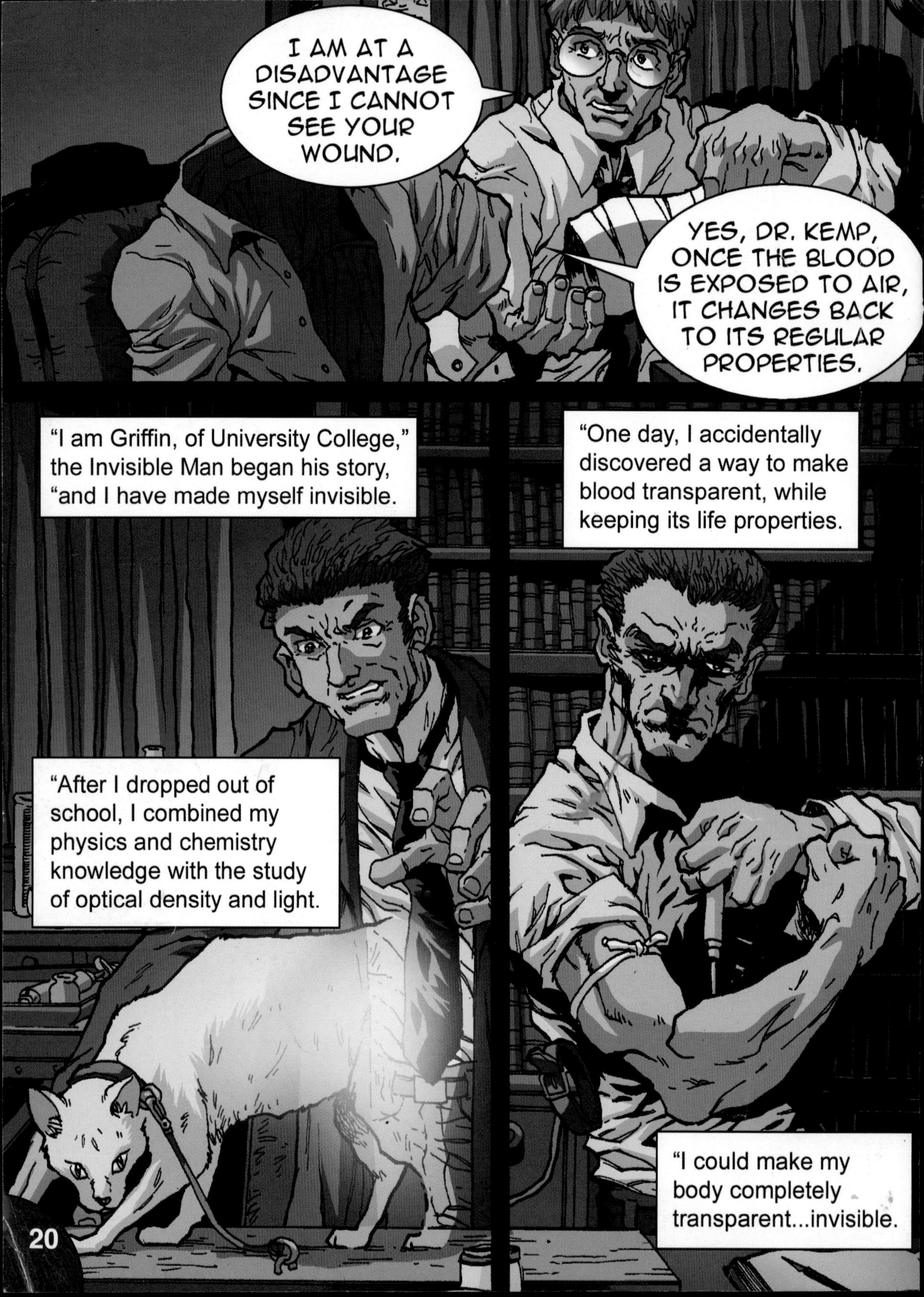
I AM AT A DISADVANTAGE SINCE I CANNOT SEE YOUR WOUND.
YES, DR. KEMP, ONCE THE BLOOD IS EXPOSED TO AIR, IT CHANGES BACK TO ITS REGULAR PROPERTIES.
"I am Griffin, of University College," the Invisible Man began his story, "and I have made myself invisible.
"After I dropped out of school, I combined my physics and chemistry knowledge with the study of optical density and light.
"One day, I accidentally discovered a way to make blood transparent, while keeping its life properties.
"I could make my body completely transparent...invisible.

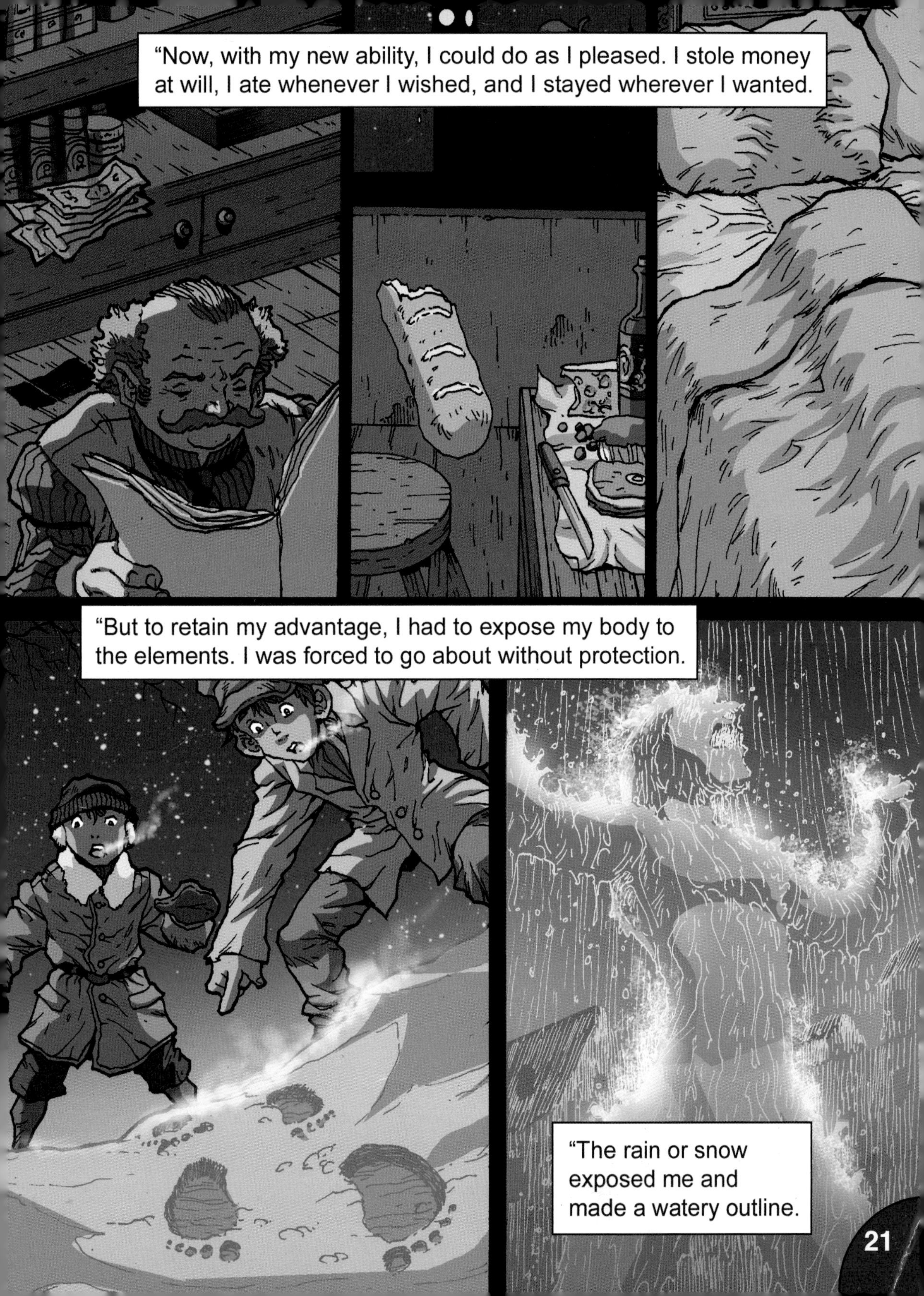
"Now, with my new ability, I could do as I pleased. I stole money at will, I ate whenever I wished, and I stayed wherever I wanted.
"But to retain my advantage, I had to expose my body to the elements. I was forced to go about without protection.
"The rain or snow exposed me and made a watery outline.

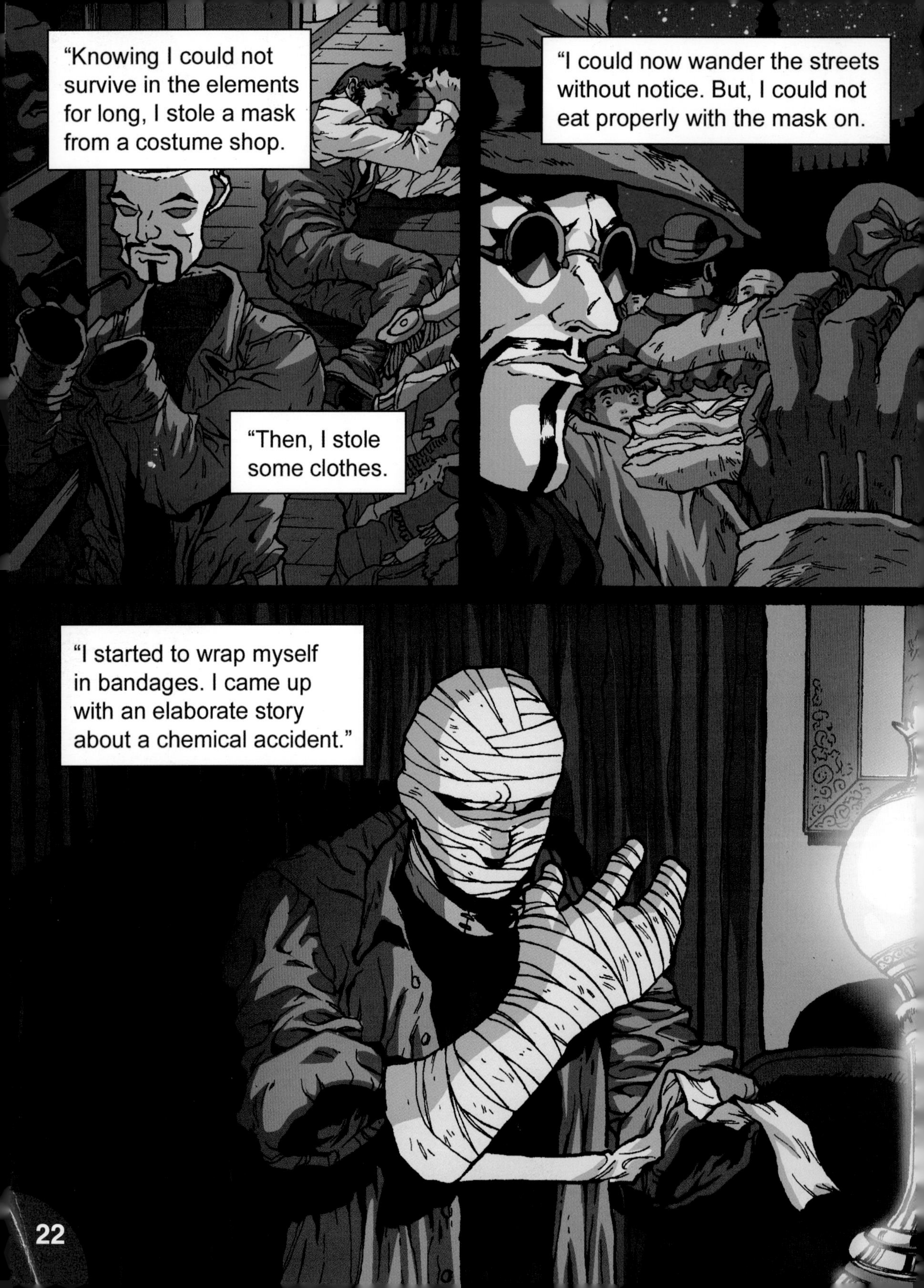
"Knowing I could not survive in the elements for long, I stole a mask from a costume shop.
"Then, I stole some clothes.
"I could now wander the streets without notice. But, I could not eat properly with the mask on.
"I started to wrap myself in bandages. I came up with an elaborate story about a chemical accident."

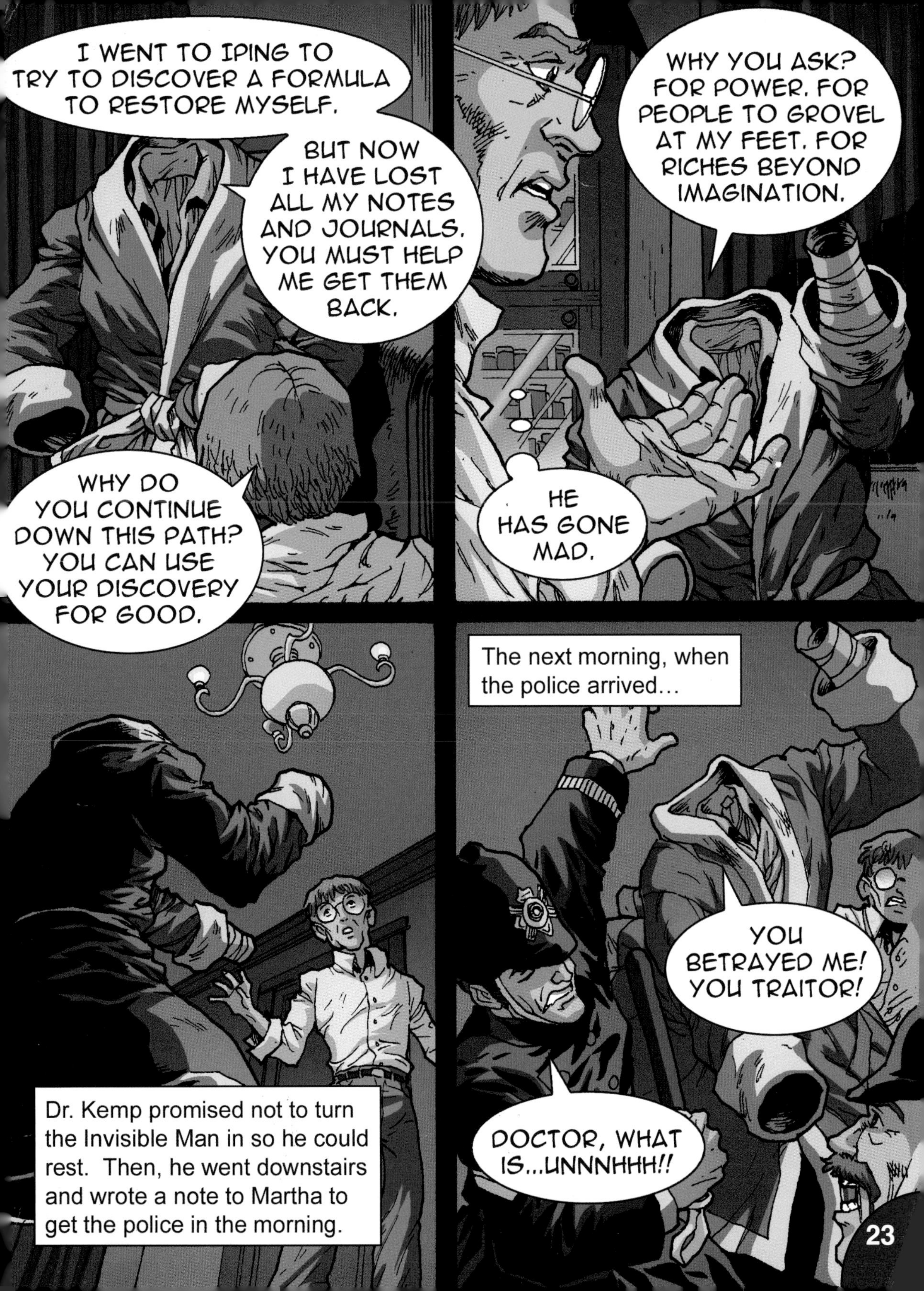

I WENT TO IPING TO TRY TO DISCOVER A FORMULA TO RESTORE MYSELF.
BUT NOW I HAVE LOST ALL MY NOTES AND JOURNALS. YOU MUST HELP ME GET THEM BACK.
WHY DO YOU CONTINUE DOWN THIS PATH? YOU CAN USE YOUR DISCOVERY FOR GOOD.
WHY YOU ASK? FOR POWER. FOR PEOPLE TO GROVEL AT MY FEET. FOR RICHES BEYOND IMAGINATION.
HE HAS GONE MAD.
Dr. Kemp promised not to turn the Invisible Man in so he could rest. Then, he went downstairs and wrote a note to Martha to get the police in the morning.
The next morning, when the police arrived…
YOU BETRAYED ME! YOU TRAITOR!
DOCTOR, WHAT IS...UNNNHHH!!

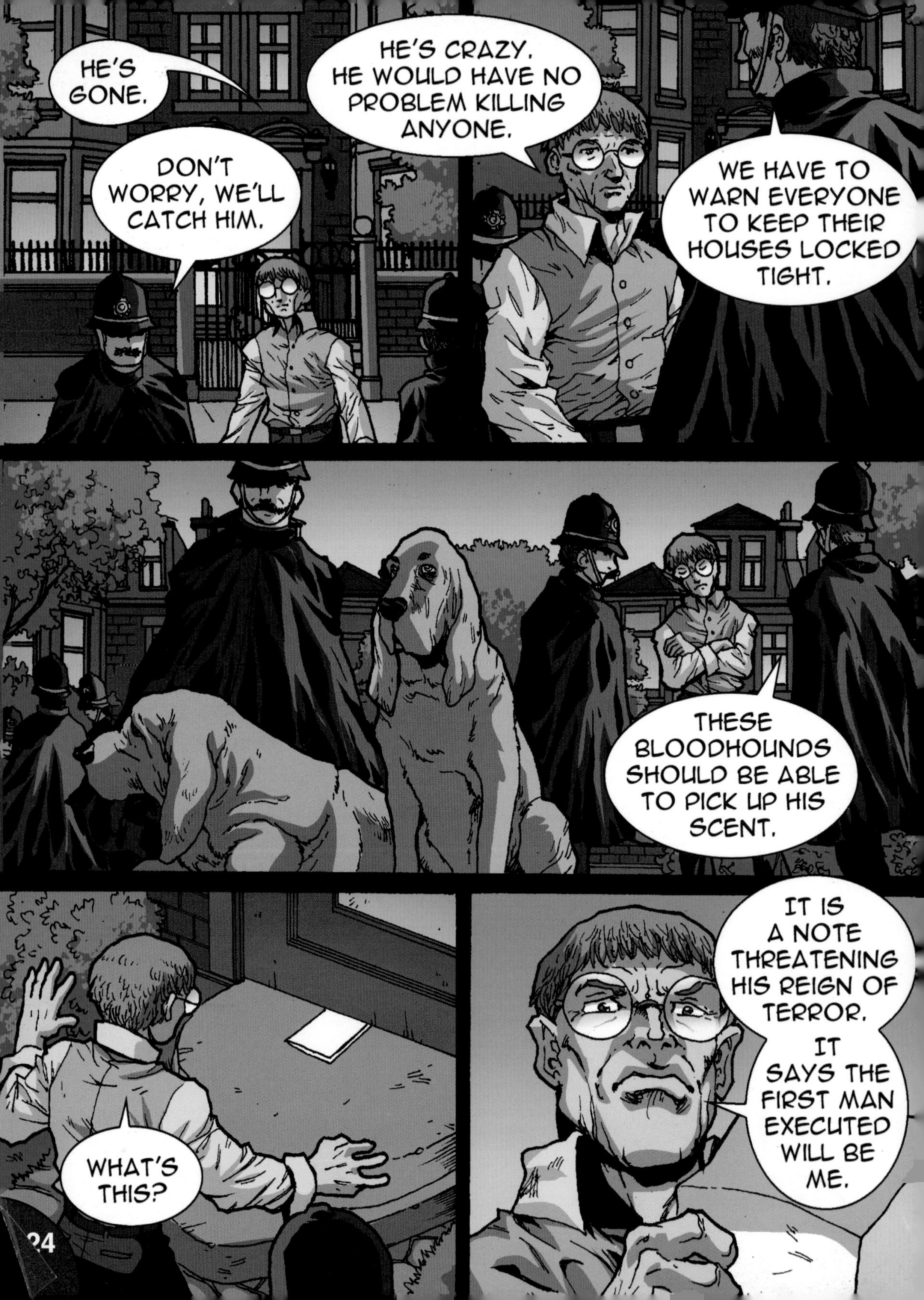
HE'S GONE.
DON'T WORRY, WE'LL CATCH HIM.
HE'S CRAZY. HE WOULD HAVE NO PROBLEM KILLING ANYONE.
WE HAVE TO WARN EVERYONE TO KEEP THEIR HOUSES LOCKED TIGHT.
THESE BLOODHOUNDS SHOULD BE ABLE TO PICK UP HIS SCENT.
WHAT'S THIS?
IT IS A NOTE THREATENING HIS REIGN OF TERROR.
IT SAYS THE FIRST MAN EXECUTED WILL BE ME.

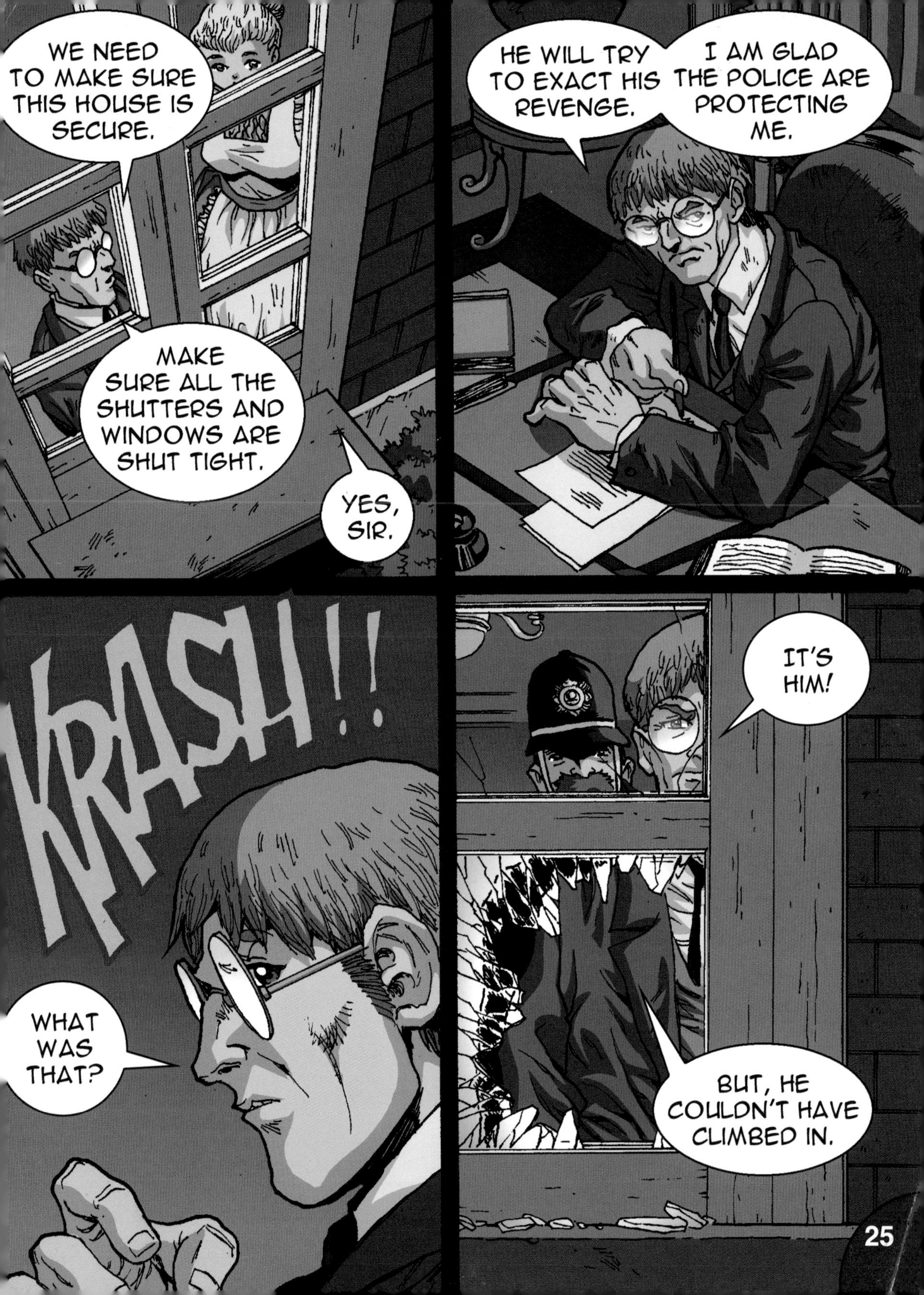
WE NEED TO MAKE SURE THIS HOUSE IS SECURE.
MAKE SURE ALL THE SHUTTERS AND WINDOWS ARE SHUT TIGHT.
YES, SIR.
HE WILL TRY TO EXACT HIS REVENGE.
I AM GLAD THE POLICE ARE PROTECTING ME.
KRASH!!
WHAT WAS THAT?
IT'S HIM!
BUT, HE COULDN'T HAVE CLIMBED IN.

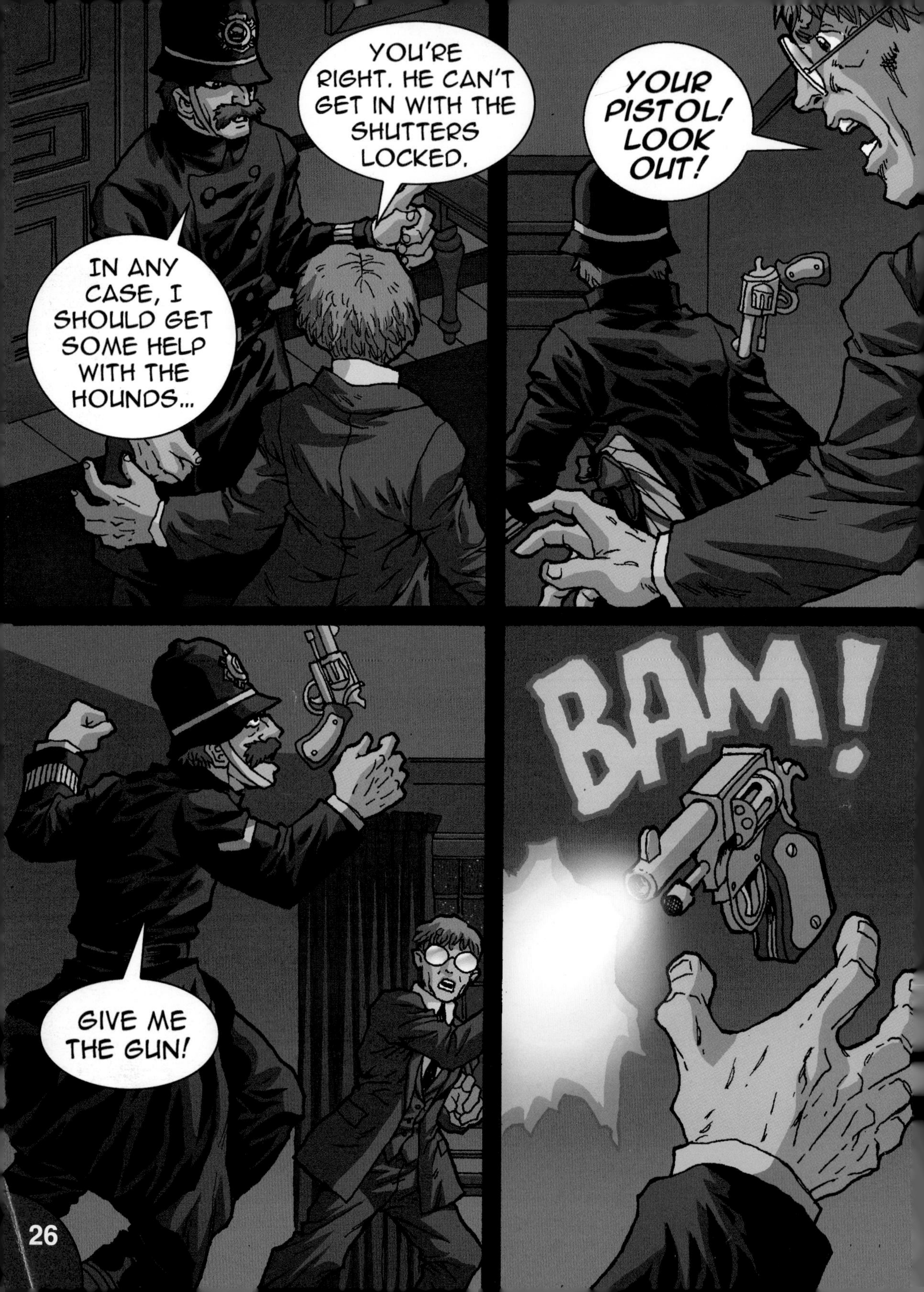

YOU'RE RIGHT. HE CAN'T GET IN WITH THE SHUTTERS LOCKED.
IN ANY CASE, I SHOULD GET SOME HELP WITH THE HOUNDS...
YOUR PISTOL! LOOK OUT!
GIVE ME THE GUN!
BAM!

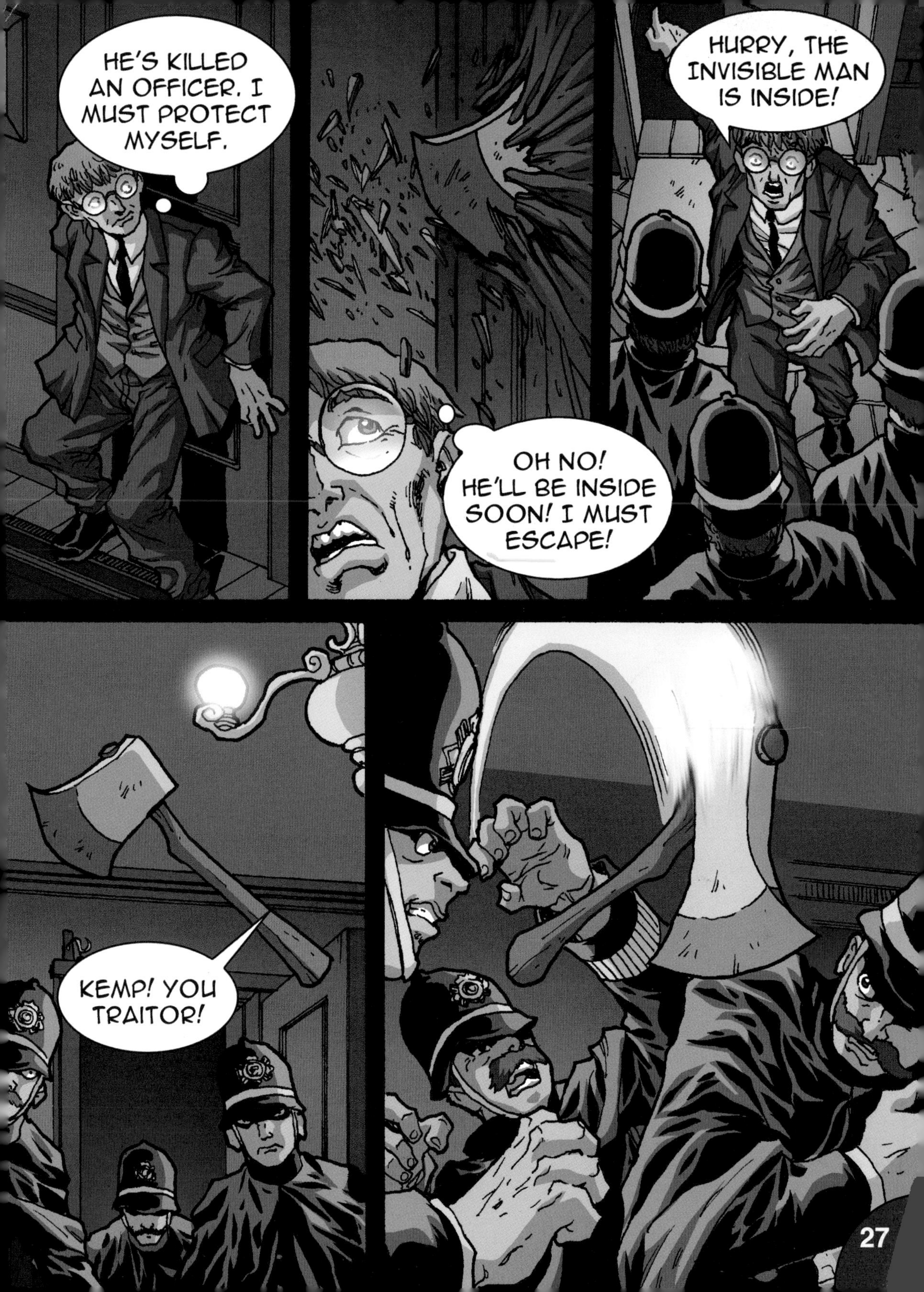
HE'S KILLED AN OFFICER. I MUST PROTECT MYSELF.
OH NO! HE'LL BE INSIDE SOON! I MUST ESCAPE!
HURRY, THE INVISIBLE MAN IS INSIDE!
KEMP! YOU TRAITOR!

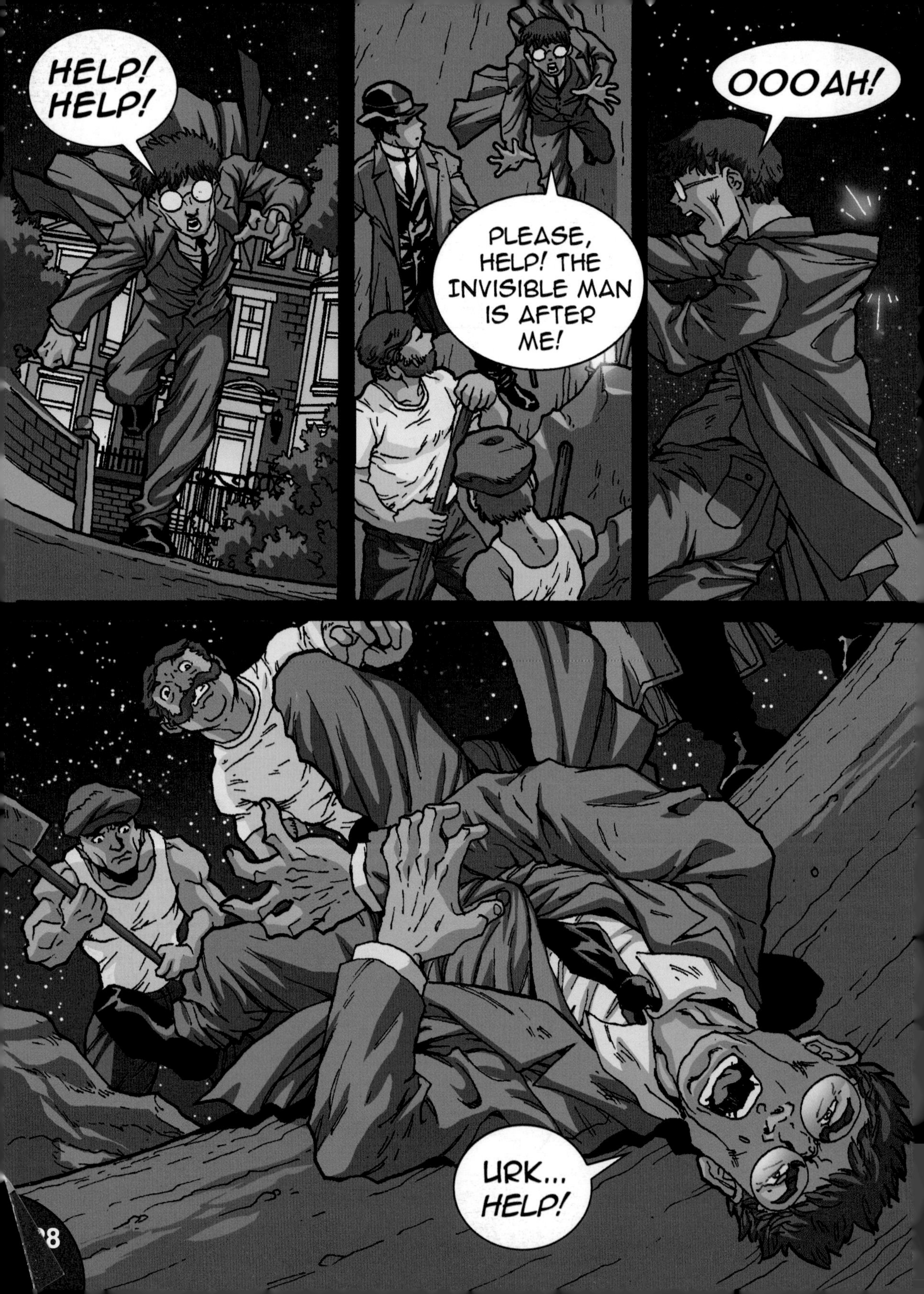
HELP! HELP!
PLEASE, HELP! THE INVISIBLE MAN IS AFTER ME!
OOOAH!
URK... HELP!

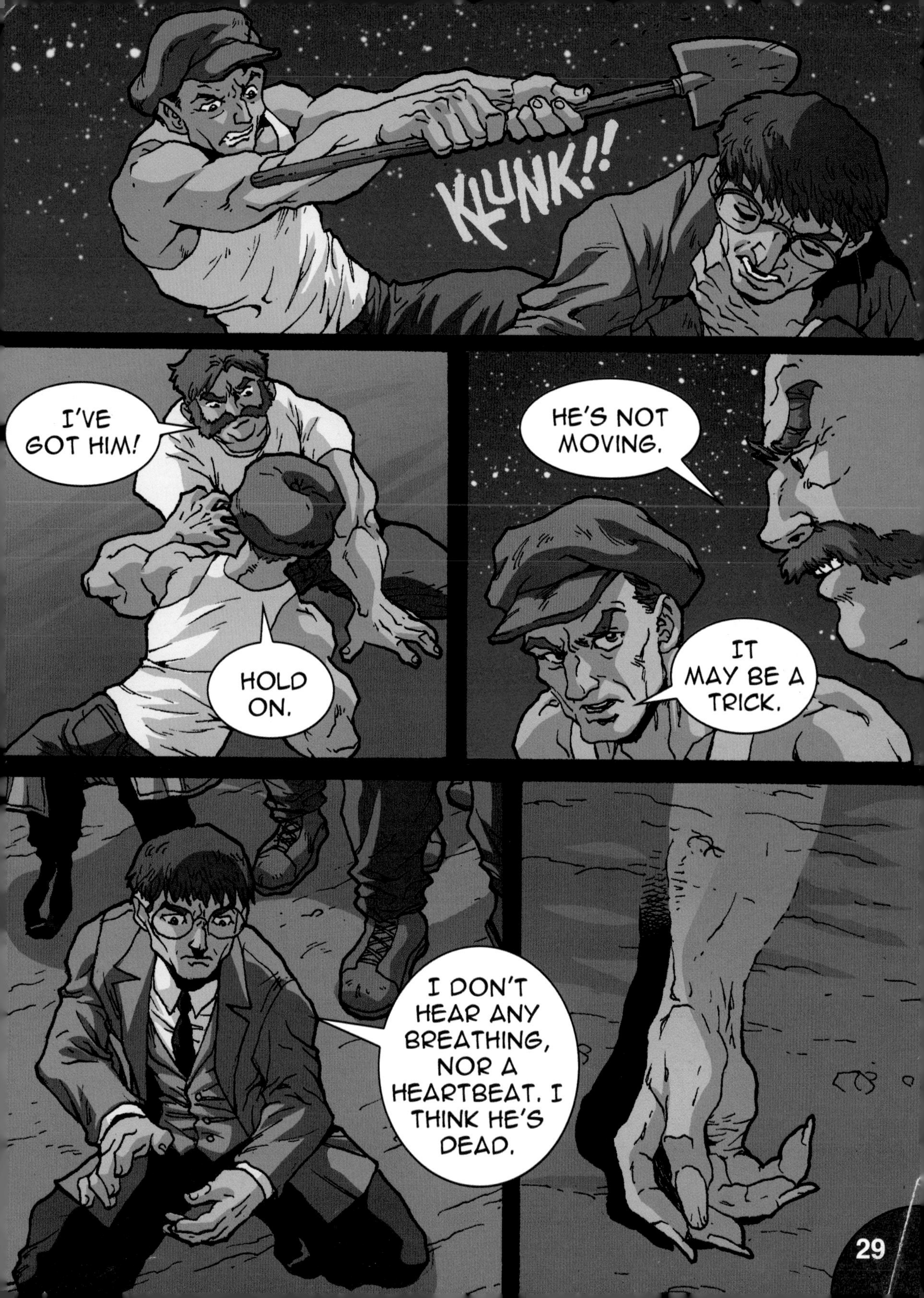
KLUNK!!
I'VE GOT HIM!
HOLD ON.
HE'S NOT MOVING.
IT MAY BE A TRICK.
I DON'T HEAR ANY BREATHING, NOR A HEARTBEAT. I THINK HE'S DEAD.

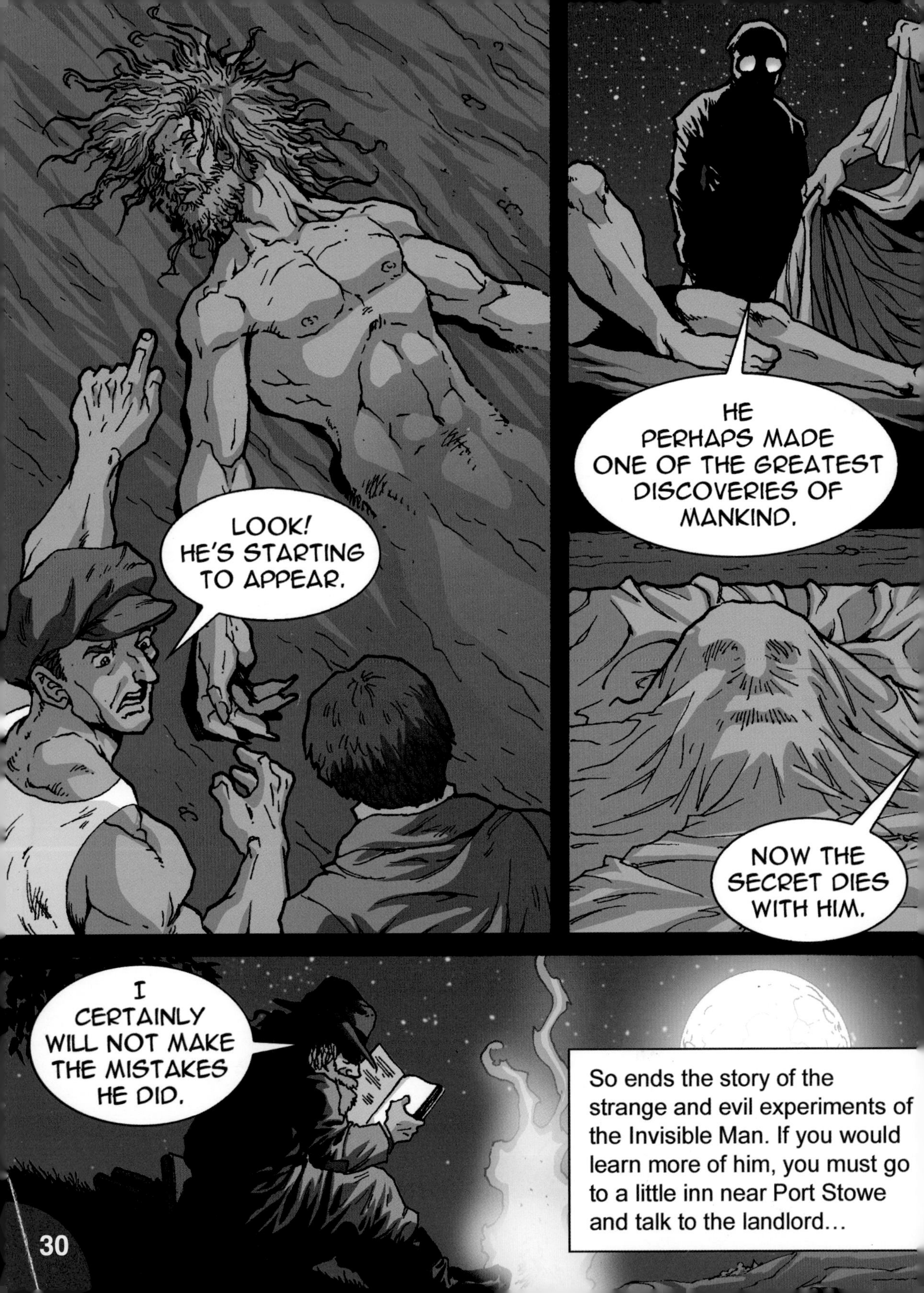
LOOK! HE'S STARTING TO APPEAR.
HE PERHAPS MADE ONE OF THE GREATEST DISCOVERIES OF MANKIND.
NOW THE SECRET DIES WITH HIM.
I CERTAINLY WILL NOT MAKE THE MISTAKES HE DID.
So ends the story of the strange and evil experiments of the Invisible Man. If you would learn more of him, you must go to a little inn near Port Stowe and talk to the landlord…

About the Author

Herbert George Wells was born in Bromley, England, on September 21, 1866. His father was a shopkeeper and his mother was a housekeeper.

H.G. attended Morley's School in Bromley, but did not get much of an education there. His real education came from reading on his own. At age 14, Wells was apprenticed to a drape maker but was soon dismissed. He then worked several jobs before becoming an aid in a grammar school.

At 18, he won a scholarship to the Royal College of Science. He graduated from the London University in 1888 and began teaching. Wells had always been interested in science fiction. Soon, he began writing it himself.

Wells added creative touches to his stories. In 1895, Wells included the idea of time as the fourth dimension in his book *The Time Machine*. This concept was not discussed or accepted until 1905, when Albert Einstein published his paper on the relativity of time!

H.G. Wells died on August 13, 1946, in London. During his lifetime he wrote many successful nonfiction works. However, it is through his great science fiction works that he is best remembered.

Additional Works

Textbook of Biology (1893)
The Time Machine (1895)
The Island of Doctor Moreau (1896)
The Invisible Man (1897)
The War of the Worlds (1898)
The First Men in the Moon (1901)
Mankind in the Making (1903)
Kipps (1905)
Mr. Britling Sees It Through (1916)
The Outline of History (1920)

Glossary

density – the quantity of anything per unit of area.

formula – a procedure to do something.

grovel – beg.

potion – a mixture of liquids.

solitude – being alone or away from other people.

transparent – easily seen through.

vicarage – the house of a vicar. A vicar is a person of the clergy.

Web Sites

To learn more about H.G. Wells, visit the ABDO Group online at **www.abdopublishing.com**. Web sites about Wells are featured on our Book Links page. These links are routinely monitored and updated to provide the most current information available.